MURDER
IN THE
CHATEAU

Also by Elliott Roosevelt

Murder in the Executive Mansion
A Royal Murder
Murder in the East Room
New Deal for Death
Murder in the West Wing
Murder in the Red Room
The President's Man
A First-Class Murder
Murder in the Blue Room
Murder in the Rose Garden
Murder in the Oval Office
Murder at the Palace
The White House Pantry Murder
Murder at Hobcaw Barony
The Hyde Park Murder
Murder and The First Lady

Perfect Crimes (ed.)

MURDER
IN THE
CHATEAU

An Eleanor Roosevelt Mystery

Elliott Roosevelt

A Thomas Dunne Book
St. Martin's Press
New York

Production Editor: David Stanford Burr

ISBN 0-312-14375-3

MURDER
IN THE
CHATEAU

I

SO MUCH ATTENTION HAS been paid to Eleanor Roosevelt's commitment to humanity and compassion in America that her dedication to world peace has been, well, not disregarded but insufficiently appreciated. Her record at the United Nations is thoroughly documented and demonstrates that late in her life her dedication to justice extended to all the peoples of the world, not just Americans. The record of her exertions and the risks she took on behalf of peace and freedom in the '30s and early '40s—which of course then meant defeat of Nazi aggression—are not well known.

The historians are not to blame. Her 1941 mission in particular remains the subject of a sealed file. It may be that no one but the late William J. Donovan, first chief of the OSS (later the CIA)—except, of course Mrs. Roosevelt herself—knew all the facts of her mission to France in the summer of 1941. Perhaps one other person knew. William Stephenson, code-named INTREPID, was intelligence liaison between the President and Winston Churchill. The mission probably originated with intelligence obtained by INTREPID, and he probably knew everything that happened.

The President himself never heard all the facts, particularly those that touched on the grave risks taken by the First Lady. The President, Churchill, INTREPID, Donovan, Secretary of War Stimson, and Secretary of State Hull were the only ones who knew even that the mission was authorized. All of them, as well as Mrs. Roosevelt, saw fit to carry the secrets to their graves.

The historians have had no way of knowing. But of course, Mrs. Roosevelt was not a completely secretive person, and eventually she did talk to someone.

The story began in April of 1941. The situation—

—France had fallen in June of 1940. Since then, the country had been divided into two parts: the north, including the city of Paris, was the German occupation zone, directly governed by the Reich government and occupied by the German army; while the south was the zone governed by a puppet French régime under the presidency of General Philippe Pétain and his collaborator prime minister, Pierre Laval. The puppet régime established its capital in the town of Vichy, so lending that part of the nation the name Vichy France.

The machinery of Nazi tyranny functioned as effectively in Vichy France as it did in Occupied France—some said even more effectively. The Gestapo, the SS, the notorious SD (*Sicherheitsdienst*, or Security Service) functioned as oppressively in Vichy France as in Occupied France, assisted by several varieties of collaborators.

The liberation of France seemed remote indeed.

—In North Africa the *Afrika Korps*, under the command of General Erwin Rommell, was at the border of Egypt and seemed likely to capture Cairo and then the Suez Canal within a month.

—The Germans, having invaded Yugoslavia and Greece, were consolidating their rule over those two countries.

—The Lend-Lease Act had been passed over the hysterical opposition of isolationists, and the first lend-lease shipments of arms to Britain were underway.

—German U-boats continued their attacks on shipping in the North Atlantic, including U.S.-flag carriers; and the President extended the American Defense Zone to the line of 26° east longitude, meaning that ships would be within that zone until they passed east of Iceland.

It was apparent to all but the most obtuse of isolationists that the United States of America was rushing toward armed conflict with Hitler's Germany. When America entered the war, the nation would want all the help it could get.

The call to a meeting in the Oval Office came as a surprise.

It was Mrs. Roosevelt's custom to stop by the President's bedroom every morning before she began her day's schedule. It was the President's custom to take breakfast in bed, eating from a tray and passing bits of food to his Scottie dog, Fala, while scanning a dozen newspapers and the morning briefing reports. Usually, too, he smoked his first Camel of the day while there in bed. Only when he had eaten his eggs and bacon and toast, drunk his coffee, and smoked that cigarette did he call his valet to help him dress and to seat him in his wheelchair for the trip downstairs and through the colonnade to the Oval Office.

She knocked, then walked in. Occasionally she would find his secretary Missy LeHand already there—or Missy *still* there; she was never sure which—but that was no longer an issue. This morning the President was alone, and she was pleased. It meant she could bring to his attention a short list of things she thought he should deal with this morning, including the issue of how Negroes were treated in the army and navy.

She was ready for a breakfast meeting that would assemble in a few minutes. She wore a wine-colored skirt and jacket with a white silk blouse and a modest string of pearls.

"Glad you stopped in, Babs," he said. "I'd have had to track you down. I'd like to see you in the Oval Office at ten-thirty. Regard the meeting as first priority and top secret."

"Franklin, I—"

"First priority and *top secret*. I suggest you cancel all your morning's appointments and eat a first-class breakfast. You're going to need to be sharp, so don't put any vodka in your breakfast orange juice."

It was his little joke, because she had never tasted vodka, and in any event would never consider drinking anything alcoholic at breakfast time.

"What is this all about, Franklin?"

"You will see," he said.

She did not cancel her breakfast appointment. She had invited a few Congressional wives for breakfast in the private dining room, and she could not reach them to cancel, even if she wanted to. She sat down over breakfast a few minutes later with Beatrice Aiken, wife of the new senator from Vermont; Claudia Johnson, called "Lady Bird," wife of one of the Texas congressmen; Nancy Kefauver, wife of one of the congressmen from Tennessee; and Bess Truman, wife of the senator from Missouri. The purpose of the breakfast meeting was to assure these women that American boys being drafted into military service were being properly taken care of: were well fed, well clothed, given proper medical attention, and, to the extent that their officers could control it, were being kept away from the brothels that were springing up in towns near training camps. A few newspapers had been publishing horror stories on all counts. For that reason, General George Marshall and his wife Katherine were also guests, and the general was prepared to answer any and all questions.

The First Lady tried to concentrate her attention on the meeting and the exchange of questions and answers, but her mind kept returning to the President's unusual summons to the Oval Office. Toward the end of the breakfast, young Miss Truman, the senator's daughter, arrived. She and her mother were going to spend the rest of the morning shopping. Mrs. Roosevelt invited her to join the group and have a cup of coffee, which the young woman did. Even Margaret Truman's bright, optimistic talk did not entirely capture the First Lady's attention. She hoped her guests did not notice how distracted she was.

At 10:30, promptly, she arrived in the West Wing and walked

through the halls to the Oval Office. Missy was looking for her and led her immediately in.

The President was seated behind his desk. He was smoking, cigarette atilt in his amber holder: a Rooseveltian trademark. Mrs. Roosevelt knew what very few visitors ever discovered, that the President's feet, which he couldn't move, were propped up on a box beneath his desk. He looked so comfortable, so confident, that even people who knew very well that he could not rise from behind that desk overlooked the dreadful fact, almost forgot it, and were sometimes momentarily surprised when he did not rise and stride across the office to shake their hands.

One man sat in a chair to the President's right.

"Babs, you know Bill," he said.

"Of course. Good morning, Bill." The President's visitor was Colonel William J. Donovan, known as "Wild Bill," and both Roosevelts had known him for many years. As a colonel in World War I, he had won the Congressional Medal of Honor as well as the Distinguished Service Cross and the Purple Heart with oak leaf cluster for being twice wounded. He was a successful New York lawyer and, being a Republican, had served in important Washington offices during the years between the wars. He had been Republican candidate for Governor of New York in 1932 and had lost to Herbert Lehman in that race to succeed Governor Roosevelt.

Lately he had earned a new title: "the President's mystery man." He had travelled to Europe repeatedly, looking into touchy questions for the President. As INTREPID was Churchill's confidential liaison with Roosevelt, Donovan was Roosevelt's to Churchill. The Prime Minister so much trusted him that Donovan and the President himself were the only Americans privy to Britain's greatest intelligence coup and secret: the breaking of the ENIGMA code.

A big, sturdy, ruddy Irishman, Donovan was a man difficult not to like. Franklin D. Roosevelt liked him and trusted him, and so did the First Lady.

She realized that whatever reason brought Donovan to the Oval Office, he was not here just to reaffirm his friendship. He was the President's covert adviser on covert operations.

"It is very good to see you, Eleanor," said Donovan. "Who'd have thought, fifteen years ago, that we would meet in this office in these circumstances?"

"Perhaps," she said, "the possibility struck me more compellingly than it did you."

He nodded and chuckled. "You may be certain of that."

"Babs," said the President, his tone ending the cordial exchange of pleasantries and summoning a graver tone, "I am sure you understand Bill has risked his life for his country recently."

"Yes," she said, speaking directly to Donovan. "I have not been privy to the secrets, but I have no doubt you have taken real risks."

"We're going to ask *you* to consider taking one, Eleanor," said Donovan.

The First Lady glanced back and forth between her husband and Donovan. She had been asked to assume political risks, maybe even personal ones, but Donovan's voice suggested that this time she was going to be asked to take a soldier's risk.

As if he read her mind, Donovan said, "A soldier's risk."

Involuntarily, she ran her tongue across her lower lip. She frowned. "I . . . have always been ready to serve my country," she said.

"Risking your life, Babs?" the President asked. "You've taken every kind of risk. You've stuck your neck out. For me. And you've taken hard knocks for it, too—more than any other First Lady has ever been asked to take. But what we're talking about is something different."

"Plus an immense responsibility," said Donovan.

"What we are saying is that we want you to feel entirely free to refuse," said the President.

"I can neither accept nor decline until I know what you are asking of me," she said.

"In a word," said the President, "I am asking you to undertake a clandestine mission to France."

"Clandestine . . . ?"

"Deep, dark, dead, dirty secret," said the President.

Mrs. Roosevelt smiled. "You mean I should be travelling incognito."

"Exactly. We will have to invent a story to explain your absence from Washington."

"Where in France am I to go? Surely not to Paris, if I am going incognito."

"You will be a guest in a château in the countryside not far from Vichy," said Donovan. "For perhaps a week. You will be an official representative of the President, speaking for him."

"Speaking to whom?" she asked.

"We will brief you exhaustively on the personalities and issues involved," said Donovan. "Among the most important of them is General Paul Rousseau. Do you know who he is?"

"He commanded an army corps, did he not? In June of 1940."

"Yes. He was one of the French generals present at the surrender ceremony at Compiègne. He was taken to Berlin, ostensibly as a guest, in fact as a hostage, and probably would have been killed if the French army had not meticulously carried out the terms of the surrender. He was in Germany about six weeks. He had no opportunity to make his way to England, as de Gaulle did. He has not suggested he wants to go to North Africa. He is living in Paris and is regarded at best as a disastrously defeated general, at worst as a traitor. What the Germans don't know—what in fact very few French people know—is that he is the center of a developing plot to bring France back into the war."

"Isn't that impossible?"

"Not necessarily," said Donovan. "A somewhat complex plot is evolving. It centers on General Rousseau, but it involves other French people: men and women, civilians as well as military. It also involves certain Germans. You must understand, Eleanor, that by no means all Germans are pleased with the Hitler régime, in spite of his spectacular victories."

"To be specific," said the President, "the key to the plot is the removal of Herr Hitler, probably by assassination, followed by an uprising in Germany. In the confusion, France would reclaim its own territory and command of its own destiny."

"Which," said Donovan, "would mean the end of the war. Even in defeat, France is still potentially the most powerful nation in Europe; and its experience of defeat and occupation by its conquerors has stiffened its back dramatically. The French are ready to fight again. All they need is opportunity, leadership, some assistance, and some very specific assurances about what Britain and the United States will do."

"Assassination . . . ?" the First Lady murmured.

"A part of your briefing," said Donovan, "will be exposure to some of the most distressing intelligence reports I have ever read. What is going on inside Germany itself but, worse, in Poland . . . Well, it is horrifying, Eleanor. In *Mein Kampf*, Hitler spoke of acquiring *Lebensraum*—living space—for the German people. Part of that territory was in Poland. So, what of the people who lived there? Eleanor, we have persuasive intelligence to the effect that the Nazis are outright murdering much of that population and enslaving the rest."

"They are killing all university professors," said the President.

"In heaven's name, *why*?" she asked.

"Natural leaders," said Donovan. "Professors. Journalists. Lawyers. Political people. Whomever the Poles might focus on as leaders of a resistance."

"Plus the Jews, by the tens of thousands," said the President.

"Jews. Jehovah's Witnesses. Freemasons. Gypsies," said Donovan. "They use machinery to dig big ditches. They strip people naked and line them up with their backs to these ditches. Then they shoot them. Many who fall into the ditches aren't dead, so the soldiers come forward and fire into the ditches. We have eyewitness accounts of this, Eleanor. It is not some isolated incident. It's happening every week."

The President shook his head. "The assassination of another

nation's head of state is contrary to everything we stand for. But in this instance—"

"You need not argue the point," said Mrs. Roosevelt. "If these reports are true, you do not need to justify yourself."

"They are true," said Donovan. "In fact, they are conservative. We are accustomed to Nazi anti-Semitism, the harassment, forfeiture of rights and property and so on. There is reason to believe that Hitler means to go much further. There is reason to believe he means to make Germany what he calls *Judenfrei*, 'free of Jews.' That may mean deporting them to Poland. It may mean something inconceivably worse."

Mrs. Roosevelt shook her head. "Surely you don't mean—"

"It could be," said Donovan grimly. "We are making every effort to find out."

The First Lady fixed a stare on the President. She nodded. "I will of course undertake this mission," she said. "I will do it, even though I cannot for the life of me imagine why it should be *me* that you want for it."

"To begin with, Babs, they asked for you," said the President.

"Partly," said Donovan, "it is a matter of commitment, of convincing the people who will be risking their lives that we are willing to take risks, too. They understand that the President can't come, so they asked for you. They understand that the Prime Minister can't come, so they asked for his son Randolph. The German representative in particular wants evidence of a full commitment."

"I suppose you have taken into consideration the idea that it might be a trap."

"Certainly we have. But the French and German representatives have demonstrated their *bona fides* in a number of ways. For example, we knew a week in advance that the Germans would invade Yugoslavia and Greece on April sixth. In reliance on that information, the British moved two battalions out of the way of the assault and deployed them to harass the German flank. The information didn't save Yugoslavia or Greece, but it saved the two battalions. Last week the British hanged a French major who had been serving on de Gaulle's staff. General Rousseau had provided conclusive evidence that the man was a German spy."

"I am asking you to become personally involved in a dangerous game," the President said to Mrs. Roosevelt. "I know you understand I wouldn't do it except for two factors: first, that Bill is assuring me the risk can be reduced to an acceptable level, second, that what we are asking you to do can become the most important thing either one of us has ever done."

Mrs. Roosevelt smiled slyly. "With that said, one could hardly refuse, could one?"

"The President spoke of an 'acceptable level' of risk," said Donovan. "The risk, I think, is more of unendurable embarrassment than of physical harm. The United States is, after all, a neutral in this war; and if the Vichy French or the Germans captured the wife of the President of the United States, I very much doubt they would do her any harm—I mean, any physical harm."

"We might be impeached, though," said the President. His tone and expression made it plain that he was not joking. He meant it. "The isolationists would howl at the moon."

"I can see the editorials now," said Mrs. Roosevelt.

"The least that would happen," said the President, "is that I would lose credibility. *We* would lose credibility. I would be seriously impeded in my efforts to assist Great Britain and save democracy in the world."

"But you think the risk is worth—?"

"There is a possibility—a remote possibility I certainly grant—that the war can be ended with little additional bloodshed. Think of it, Babs. A coup in Berlin, Hitler dead or imprisoned, Germany in turmoil as it was at the end of 1918, occupation troops called home to try to restore order, the French rearmed and reorganized— Maybe I am too enthusiastic, but the possibility, even the possibility, is just too important not to pursue."

"Something else, Eleanor," said Donovan. "In August of 1939, Hitler and Stalin signed a neutrality pact. You know what followed. Confident that the Soviet Union would not oppose him, Hitler invaded Poland. Okay. A couple of days ago Stalin signed a neutrality pact with Japan. Now . . . Freed from the necessity of worrying about a Russian attack on their forces in Manchuria and China, the Japanese can now look to— Well, to what? French Indo-China? Malaya? The Dutch East Indies? To sources of oil and rubber and rice."

"If Germany falls apart," said the President, "the British and French and Dutch will be able to reinforce their garrisons in Southeast Asia. That could mean peace in the Pacific."

"It would mean the perpetuation of colonialism," she said.

"As between European colonialism and Japanese imperialism, what's to choose?" asked Donovan. "The Japanese don't exploit their colonies with gentle hands."

The President had pulled the butt of his cigarette from his holder, and now he inserted a fresh one and lit it. "It's a long shot," he said. "It's a long, long shot. But this scheme offers a chance of heading off the war before it spreads farther. I know you understand that we will not be able to stay out of it if it expands any more."

"Another point," said Donovan. "Hitler may be planning to invade Russia. Suppose he does, and suppose he defeats Russia and adds all its resources to what he already has. Where do we stop him then?"

"You need not plead your case further, gentlemen. I am prepared to undertake this mission. My remaining concern is that I shall be *able* to perform my duties."

"You speak French," said the President. "That is going to help."

"How are we going to explain my absence?"

"I must tell you in the first place," said Donovan, "that we are not quite certain when you will be needed in France. General Rousseau must have some occasion to cross the demarcation line between Occupied France and Vichy. The Germans must suppose he is going for some ceremonial or similar reason. He is trying to work out an invitation from Marshal Pétain. Also, the German officer may have some difficulty getting away from his duties."

"In any event, you must go on to California for Jimmy's wedding," said the President. "That you are going has been announced, and a change in that plan would raise suspicions."

"I suspect it may be the first of June before you are called on," said Donovan. "You will need that much time to be briefed."

"I am a quick study, Bill," she said.

"I have no doubt. But you must be thoroughly familiar with a thousand details. I would like to send your first briefing officer with you on the flight to California. You will have many hours of free time on the plane, and she can get you started."

"She?"

"A highly competent young woman. She will in fact be accompanying you to France, as will a young man. She speaks fluent German as well as French. Her name is . . . Well, let us not say. She will travel with you as Victoria Klein."

"Are you telling me that a young Jewish woman will be going to France with me? Isn't that a frightful risk for her to take?"

"It is a risk that she is more than willing to take. And she will have a role in the mission, as you will see."

"Her ostensible role is that of your personal maid," said the President. "Beginning with the flight to California, she will act that role. Even General Rousseau will not know who she is."

"And the young man?" asked Mrs. Roosevelt.

"We haven't settled on the man, for sure," said Donovan.

"And how am I to travel to France? I've heard of the black-painted airplanes that land on remote fields."

"That's not settled for sure, either," said Donovan. "I do promise you one thing, Eleanor." He paused to grin. "We will not ask you to make a parachute jump."

The President laughed. "We might," he said. "But whatever method we use must not only get you safely into France but safely out again. The trouble with parachuting is that you can parachute down all right, but you can't parachute *up*."

"You can if the winds are strong enough, I promise you," said Donovan.

"That's amusing, I suppose, but—"

"Eleanor . . ." said Donovan soberly. "We spoke of acceptable risk. So far as I am concerned, that means minimal risk. There are scores of officials, many of the Vichy government, some even of the German government, willing to give you a safe crossing of the border."

"Switzerland?" she asked.

"Afraid not. The Swiss are so determined to maintain their neutrality that they would block us on *their* side of the crossing. You couldn't possibly fly into Switzerland without being identified. No, I'm afraid that's out. It may be possible from Spain or even from Italy. We're working on it. But we'll find a safe way to do it—or we won't do it at all."

"Amen," said the President.

NOT UNTIL MONDAY, JUNE 9, did Mrs. Roosevelt receive word as to when and how she was to go to France.

The intervening weeks had been eventful.

—On the night of May 10–11, the Deputy Leader of the Nazi Party, Rudolf Hess, flew solo from Germany to Britain and parachuted into a field near Glasgow. He announced he had come as the Führer's special representative, to arrange the end of hostilities between Britain and Germany and form an alliance for joint operations against the Soviet Union. Hitler denounced him and declared him a traitor.

—On that same night, German bombers severely damaged the House of Commons. Then, mysteriously, the bombers stopped coming. No one in Britain could have guessed it, but that was the last major raid of the Blitz. The Battle of Britain was finally and decisively won.

—On May 11 the American merchant ship *Robin Moore* was sunk by a German U-boat within the American Defense Zone proclaimed by the President only a month before. On the 27th the President declared a state of unlimited national emergency.

—On May 23, the German battleship *Bismarck*, escorted by the heavy cruiser *Prinz Eugen*, escaped German waters and sortied into the North Atlantic, where immediately it sank the British battleship *Hood. Hood* went down with 1458 men. *Bismarck* was, however, hit in a fuel tank and left a trail of fuel oil. On the 27th, British air and naval forces caught up with it as it dashed for a French port for repairs. Torpedoed by British aircraft, then by destroyers, and shot to pieces by British battleships, *Bismarck* sank.

Mrs. Roosevelt had flown to Los Angeles to attend the wedding of her son James. She stayed only for the wedding and flew immediately to New York.

The President had stayed in Washington and had tossed out the first ball to open the American League baseball season. The New York Yankees defeated the Washington Senators 3 to 0.

In New York, Mrs. Roosevelt attended a performance of Lillian Hellman's play *Watch on the Rhine.* Ten days later she was again in Los Angeles, for a real visit with her new daughter-in-law. She was the guest of the actor Melvyn Douglas during this visit, and among the guests he invited to see her were Burgess Meredith, Dorothy Parker, and Thomas Mann.

During these travels, the young woman she was to call Victoria Klein accompanied her. Every hour they had alone was devoted to a review of documents and photographs, plus extensive commentary by Miss Klein, until the First Lady felt certain she would recognize at sight anyone she was likely to meet in France—and would know that person's biography, politics, religion, and philosophy. In addition, Miss Klein drilled her in a new French that Mrs. Roosevelt had not dreamed was spoken, replete with grammatical *gaucheries* Miss Klein insisted had become commonplace in the language since those long-ago days when the young Eleanor Roosevelt had studied French with Mademoiselle Souvestre at Allenswood school in England. Besides that, Mrs. Roosevelt needed to know the new French idioms and slang, plus the terminology of the German occupation and the Vichy régime.

And there was more. They spent many intense hours together.

Victoria Klein was a slight young woman, a full foot shorter than Mrs. Roosevelt. She parted her dark-brown hair in the middle and allowed it to hang smoothly down to her shoulders and indeed ten or more inches down her back—so it was distinctly unstylish and drew glances from people everywhere. She was beautiful. There was no point in describing her any other way; she was simply beautiful, in a distinctive way. Her face, her complexion especially, suggested Oriental ancestry, not Far Eastern probably but Middle Eastern. Her unplucked eyebrows were heavy. Her nose was uptilted and delicate. Her mouth was characterized by a lower lip that was fleshy and protruded a little—which only made her the more beautiful. She was highly introspective, Mrs. Roosevelt observed. In quiet moments she lowered her eyes, adopted a private, enigmatic smile, and seemed to withdraw. Her English was British English, which she spoke with a German accent. Mrs. Roosevelt supposed, and hoped, her French was not similarly accented.

She played her role perfectly. She was the maid. To Mrs. Roosevelt's surprise, she carried maid's uniforms in her baggage; and when they were settled in a hotel suite or in the quarters provided for them by Melvyn Douglas in his Hollywood home, Victoria donned a black or gray dress, with a little white apron and a white starched cap. She was deferential always, but when others were present she spoke only very quietly, called Mrs. Roosevelt nothing but "Ma'am," and busied herself attending to every possible requirement the First Lady might have.

The true nature of the relationship was dramatically demonstrated when the First Lady discovered that her pretty, deferential little maid carried a gun.

Mrs. Roosevelt knew virtually nothing about firearms. Victoria explained to her that the tiny automatic she carried was what Americans called a "Baby Browning." It was a 6.35 mm—that is, .25 caliber—six-shot pistol. She carried it in a soft leather holster under her left arm; and, as she demonstrated, she could quickly reach inside whatever she was wearing and pull it out.

"But why do you carry it, Miss Klein?" Mrs. Roosevelt asked.

"I will tell you if you will call me Vicky." In her accent it came out, "I veel tell you if you veel call me Veeky."

"I am reluctant to use first names on short acquaintance," said the First Lady. "Anyway, Vicky is not your real name."

Victoria's chin rose abruptly. She stiffened defiantly. "I will tell you my name," she said. "It is not a secret from you. But you must never use it, not even when we think we are completely alone. We will be places where there may be hidden microphones. You should call me Vicky. Ladies do not call their maids 'Miss.' Since we can never know if we are overheard, I am Vicky, and you must treat me like a servant. I will call you 'Mrs. Roosevelt' or 'Ma'am.' My real name is Viktoria Neustadt. Someday we will talk about who that is."

Mrs. Roosevelt nodded agreement. "I will do as you say. But, still, why the pistol?"

"Who knows what may happen? Before we leave for France, you are going to learn to fire a gun, and when we go you will be carrying one. God forbid we should ever have to use them."

"I don't think I wish to carry one."

Victoria smiled. "You have enlisted as a soldier, so to speak. I think our commanding officers are going to insist on it."

On the evening of Thursday, May 29, the President addressed a gathering of Western Hemisphere diplomats in the East Room. His address was broadcast to the nation.

The flags of all the American nations decorated the East Room. The President sat at a desk facing a battery of more than a dozen microphones. Scores of reporters and cameramen faced him. The diplomats sat respectfully listening. The President spoke for three-quarters of an hour, reviewing the world situation and emphasizing the vital role hemispheric solidarity might have in gaining the ultimate defeat of the Nazis.

"We will not accept a Hitler-dominated world," the President said firmly. He cited Winston Churchill's speech of a month before, in which the Prime Minister had referred to the Germans as "the malignant Huns" and Mussolini as a "whipped jackal."

The American diplomats applauded the President's speech,

and then Irving Berlin rose to sing his song "God Bless America." After the guests left the White House, Berlin stayed and sang songs for the President and Mrs. Roosevelt and a few friends, in the Monroe Room.

The First Lady might have enjoyed the music more—might indeed have enjoyed the speech more—if she had not spent almost two hours that afternoon at Fort McNair, in the officers' indoor pistol range, learning to handle and fire a pistol. Her ears still rang with the explosions of the cartridges.

Vicky had been right in suggesting that Donovan and even the President himself would demand that she carry a gun when she went to France. Mrs. Roosevelt did not understand that requirement and was not in sympathy with it, but she decided she had better learn to handle a pistol, in case she lost the argument.

She had decided, too, that this mission might require more rugged and serviceable clothes than her usual dresses and suits. She'd had made, therefore, three outfits in a style she would later adopt and wear commonly when she travelled to military and naval bases and hospitals in the South Pacific and elsewhere: skirts and jackets of khaki twill. She wore one of these outfits with a cotton blouse when she went to the pistol range.

Her presence there that afternoon was no secret. Still, the officers left the range when she entered, accompanied by a young captain and by Vicky Klein.

At first Mrs. Roosevelt's hand trembled when she took an unloaded revolver in her hand. She could not recall ever having touched a handgun before. She had always regarded them as threatening objects, useful only for the purpose of injuring or killing another person, and she had wanted nothing to do with them. After the officer had explained to her the trigger and the safety and how to handle the weapon without risking injury to herself and others around her, she felt no different: the thing was dangerous and serviceable only for doing harm.

Even so, she was a quick study, as she had told Donovan, and

within five minutes understood how to load the revolver, to set the safety, to keep the muzzle pointed away from herself and others, and how to aim and fire.

What the captain called a Colt revolver fired what he called .38 caliber ammunition. He handed her six cartridges and told her to load. Reluctantly, the First Lady pushed the brass-and-lead objects into what he called the chambers. She shoved the cylinder into place; and, nervously conscious that she now had a loaded revolver in hand, set the safety.

"Now, Ma'am. Aim at the target, please, and fire one shot. Remember you don't jerk the trigger. Squeeze it gently."

Mrs. Roosevelt filled her lungs with breath, steadied herself, and pointed the barrel of the pistol toward the target on a wall of heavy lumber, fifty feet away. She squeezed the trigger. It wouldn't budge.

"Release the safety," said Vicky gently.

The First Lady smiled nervously and pressed down on the little lever. Now she squeezed the trigger again. The hammer came back, then abruptly snapped forward. The cartridge exploded, the pistol barked loudly and bucked, almost enough to jerk itself out of her hand, and the report of the shot echoed harshly off the brick walls: a deafening noise.

"All right," said the captain. "You didn't hit the target, but you didn't shoot your foot off, either. Let's do it again. Just be steady. Don't let it frighten you. Hold your sights on the target until you're ready, then fire."

Mrs. Roosevelt was a tall woman and physically strong. Her height and husky physique had caused her to be called uncomplimentary things: gawky being the kindest of them. Since she couldn't be a shrinking violet, no matter how much she might have wished to, she wondered if she might not as well take advantage of being what she was.

"Is it improper," she asked the captain, "to grasp my right wrist with my left hand, so gaining additional steadiness?"

The captain nodded his head. "We don't let our lieutenants do it when they're qualifying with the .45, but I can't think of a reason why you shouldn't."

She nodded. It seemed a sensible way to make a steadier aim. Mrs. Roosevelt closed her left hand around her right wrist. She fixed the sights on the black circle, the bull's-eye, and squeezed again.

Vicky was staring at the target through a small telescope mounted on a tripod. "Seven," she said. "Damn good!"

"Another?" asked Mrs. Roosevelt.

The captain nodded, and she aimed and fired her third shot.

"Five," said Vicky.

"You've got three more. Finish them."

The First Lady set her legs apart for even more steadiness, aimed grimly, and fired three more shots in the next fifteen seconds.

"Two, eight, six," said Vicky. "That's very good, Ma'am. That's good for anybody."

Mrs. Roosevelt rolled the cylinder out and expelled the empty cartridges. She still didn't like the pistol, but she wasn't quite so afraid of it. Her ears rang. "All right?" she asked. "Is that it?"

"I'd like to ask you to fire a few more rounds, Ma'am," said the captain. "We can fine-tune you a little. Then we'll put away the big revolver, and I'll introduce you to the kind of pistol I was asked to introduce you to."

Her scores for the first six shots had added up to twenty-eight, in spite of the fact that only five shots had been in the target at all. To her frustration, her next six shots and the six after that never totalled twenty-eight. Her final six totalled thirty-one.

Then the game changed. The captain took down the bull's-eye target and put up a life-size black-on-white silhouette of a man, only about ten feet away.

"I really don't want to shoot at that," Mrs. Roosevelt said.

"I'm sorry, Ma'am. My orders are to introduce you to a small pocket automatic, and you would never hit a bull's-eye target at fifty feet with that."

Vicky spoke to the captain. "Would you mind stepping outside for a moment?" she asked. Then she turned to Mrs. Roosevelt. "Ma'am . . ." she said. "Watch."

She reached down in her dress, drew her Baby Browning, and, firing from the hip, put six quick shots into the chest area of the silhouette.

The First Lady shook her head. "You have proved you are capable of killing a man," she said.

"I've proved I am capable of saving my life and maybe saving yours. I've never killed anybody. I never will, except to save myself, or maybe save you or someone else. But I want to be sure I can. I would like to think you could save *my* life if the situation arose. I'd like to think at least that you wouldn't shrink from it, on pacifist principle."

Mrs. Roosevelt nodded. "Very well. Let's call the captain in and see what he proposes to teach me."

He handed her a small automatic. It was not like Vicky's but was a .32 caliber Colt, small enough to be called a pocket pistol, yet considerably bigger than the Baby Browning. She was less successful with that. He assured her that was what he had expected. Firing a small automatic from the hip, he said, was far, far less accurate than firing a revolver extended with two arms. Still, she managed to steady herself; and, in spite of her distaste for the exercise, she learned how to load, cock, and fire the Colt. She fired sixty rounds; and by the end she was putting four or five shots out of six somewhere on the silhouette.

"I congratulate you, Ma'am," said the captain before she left. "When I was told who my student on the firing range was to be, I couldn't imagine you could do it at all. Not that I thought you'd be incapable. No. I just suspected a lady like yourself wouldn't be able to overcome your distaste for this sort of thing. But you did. You're not bad. With practice, you could be a lot better. I do beg one thing, Ma'am. Be careful. Always be careful. A loaded gun is dangerous."

"That was my point," said Mrs. Roosevelt with a smile. "Thank you, Captain. And good-bye."

The next day she was introduced to a radio transceiver in a small leather case that looked like—in fact, had been—a case for a lady's combs, brushes, and manicure set. This radio could receive signals from anywhere in the world. It could transmit more than five hundred miles. Vicky tuned it and listened for a minute or so, then handed the earphones to Mrs. Roosevelt, who listened and heard the dah-dits of Morse code. She then taught the First Lady to use the key to transmit dahs and dits.

"I am going to give you a short coded message," said Vicky. "You must memorize it. Then you should practice tapping it out on the key. It is our emergency signal, calling for help. It could happen that *you* will have to transmit it."

Mrs. Roosevelt nodded. The mission was beginning to take on a somber note, one that she had anticipated but which was distressing nevertheless now that it began to develop.

"The message is a number, followed by a question mark. Okay? 2391? That's 1932, the year the President was first elected, backwards. Then question mark. I'll write out the Morse code."

Vicky wrote—

● ● ─ ─ ─	● ● ● ─ ─	─ ─ ─ ─ ●	● ─ ─ ─ ─	● ● ─ ─ ● ●
2	3	9	1	?

"Before we leave for France the tuning coil will be replaced by a crystal, so we'll be able to transmit and receive on one frequency only. That frequency will be constantly monitored, by at least five stations. If you have to send the message, repeat it just once. Send it and repeat it. Then switch off the power. Remember, the Nazis will be listening, too. You don't want to transmit long enough to let them get a fix with a direction finder. That's why it's important to practice. You should be able to transmit the message in less than fifteen seconds. Then again, that's thirty seconds, then off the air."

"What, exactly, does the message mean?" asked Mrs. Roosevelt.

"It means we are in deep trouble and need immediate rescue. A rescue plan has been made. God forbid we have to be rescued, but if we do, there is a plan for it."

"What does the plan involve?"

"An attack on the château by *résistants.*"

A little later in the day, Vicky brought to the First Lady's office a telegraph key attached to a small, battery-powered beeper. That evening and for several evenings thereafter, Mrs. Roosevelt practiced at sending 2391?—until she was able to tap out the dits and dahs crisply in twelve seconds. Vicky listened to her occasionally and encouraged her.

Mrs. Roosevelt did not tell Vicky, but she also memorized the full Morse code and practiced a little at sending other messages. Who could tell what might develop?

On Monday afternoon, June 9, a message came up from the Oval Office. The President would like to see Mrs. Roosevelt as soon as possible. She went down. Donovan was with the President. She knew what they were going to say before they said it.

"Got your bags packed?" the President asked.

"I believe I am prepared."

The President nodded. "Day after tomorrow," he said. He was solemn. His cigarette lay aside, burning in an ashtray. "It's not too late to change your mind. It's not too late for any of us to change our minds."

She shook her head firmly. "No, Franklin, I will not change my mind. I know there is risk, but the opportunity is so great that it must be pursued, no matter what the risk."

"We have prepared a story as to where you are going to be," said the President. "We'll issue a statement to the press on Wednesday, to the effect that you have caught the flu and will be laid up for a few days. Dr. Grayson will issue bulletins on you, that your flu is a little more persistent than anticipated but that you are resting comfortably and gradually improving. You may want to bolster the story by coughing a few times in public in the next few days."

"I have written enough advance 'My Day' columns to cover two weeks," she said.

"The mission may take a little longer than that," said Donovan.

"In which case my ostensible illness will be a handy excuse for missing a few columns," she said. "I have left them with Tommy Thompson. She will have to be told that I am not in fact ill but am travelling on a confidential mission. She needn't of course be told where I am or why?"

"No, and Dr. Grayson will not be told either," said Donovan.

"Who *has* been made privy to the secret?" she asked.

"Cordell Hull and Henry Stimson," said the President. "And Winston Churchill."

"I have another question," said Mrs. Roosevelt. "Exactly who is Vicky Klein? She has told me her real name, so I do know that much. But I feel I should know a bit more about her if I am to entrust so much to her."

"Has she made a good impression?" Donovan asked.

"An excellent impression."

"Good. Her name is Viktoria Neustadt. Her father was a Viennese lawyer. Her brother was studying law. The family is of course Jewish. When the Nazis took over Austria, the family suffered horribly, first humiliation, then far worse. They were all arrested. Viktoria and her mother were eventually released, but she has had no word from her father or brother and doesn't even know if they are alive. The stress killed her mother. She had a heart attack and died. With the assistance of some other Jews, Viktoria escaped from Austria, into Switzerland, then into France. She was in Paris when the German troops arrived. She fled south. Then she found out she wasn't safe in Vichy either. The Pétain-Laval government has been prodded into a policy of vicious anti-Semitism. So Viktoria joined the *Résistance*. And that's what she is: a *résistante*. She is also a personal representative of General Rousseau, assigned by him to bring you to France. She will not be coming back with you when the mission is over."

"What about the young man who is to accompany me?"

"You will meet him during the voyage," said the President.

"I have something for you," said Donovan. He opened his briefcase and withdrew a Baby Browning automatic, exactly like the one carried by Vicky. It was encased in a soft leather holster, also just like the one Vicky wore. He handed it to her with two extra clips of ammunition. "I hope it turns out to be nothing but a nuisance," he said.

Mrs. Roosevelt frowned over the pistol. "I am not sure I wish to have this," she said.

"Please carry it, Babs," said the President. "I will pray you never have to use it, but I don't want you to be without it."

"Very well," she sighed. She dropped pistol, holster, and extra ammunition into her purse. "So . . . So how are we to travel to France?"

Donovan shook his head and smiled wryly. "In some discomfort," he said.

THEY LEFT THE WHITE House well before dawn on Wednesday, June 11: Mrs. Roosevelt and Victoria Klein. Two Secret Service men sat in the front seat of a Cadillac belonging to the Department of War. The two women sat in back. The trunk was crammed with their luggage—crammed because the First Lady's trip was a diplomatic mission, and she had to expect formal dinners and luncheons.

"I can't remember ever having felt quite so silly," said Mrs. Roosevelt to Vicky as the car sped through Maryland.

To maintain an incognito, she was dressed as she never dressed: in high-heel, open-toe shoes and a bright-red belted cotton dress, with dark sunglasses, her hair tied up in a rayon scarf. Vicky was dressed similarly, except that her dress was yellow.

Their Secret Service driver and bodyguard knew the tall woman in the back seat was the First Lady. They knew where they were taking her, but they didn't know why, and they had no idea who the younger, smaller woman might be.

Since the two men in the front seat knew nothing of the mission, the women could not talk about it. Vicky stared thoughtfully at the towns and countryside through which they passed, acquainting herself with another aspect of America. Mrs. Roosevelt spent much of her time studying a highway map of France, also reading a history provided by Donovan of the château they were going to visit.

The highway, U.S. 1, carried them through Baltimore, then Philadelphia, and then on north through New Jersey toward New York City. The First Lady took some pride in the road, since much widening and straightening and paving had been done as W.P.A. projects, so giving thousands of unemployed men work and giving the nation a fine modern highway—some of it three, and a few miles of it even four, lanes. It made it possible for them to reach New York in less than eight hours.

In fact, they were able to reach the seaplane terminal in the East River well before noon, the scheduled takeoff time.

Their airplane, a huge, four-engine Pan American flying boat, was moored at a floating dock that rose and fell with the tide. It looked something like an immense whale rocking gently on the waves, straining at its mooring ropes like a small ship. The high wing was long and tapered, painted on top with a tapering orange stripe. The engines hung beneath the wing and extended well forward. Besides the usual fin standing above the rear of the body of the airplane, the flying boat had two more, mounted at the ends of the stabilizer. Staring at the machine, Mrs. Roosevelt found it hard to believe that anything so large and ungainly in appearance could ever lift itself off the water and fly. She knew though that this type of airplane, technically designated a Boeing B-314, flew regular service across both the Atlantic and Pacific Oceans.

This one was leaving at noon for Lisbon. Since the United States and Portugal were neutral countries, there was no danger of interference from warplanes. Transatlantic service, New York to Lisbon and return, was offered three times a week. Occasionally in winter, when heavy ice floated on the East River, the Clipper, as it was called, landed at Miami.

A blue-and-white-striped awning covered the wooden walkway, and Mrs. Roosevelt and Vicky walked down to the dock. It had been necessary to trust three members of the flight crew with the identity of their famous passenger, so they were greeted on the dock by the captain.

"There are no other passengers aboard," he said. "You can walk right through the plane to your cabin, and no one will see you."

Mrs. Roosevelt glanced back and noticed that the rest of the passengers had been kept in the terminal until the special passengers arrived. Feeling uncomfortably self-conscious, she stepped through the entry door and into the spacious interior of the Clipper.

Consciously appointed like the first-class accommodations on a liner, the airplane was furnished with wide leather seats, half of them facing rearward. Walking through the first passenger cabin, they entered a galley and bar, behind which was another passenger cabin and then the dining room and lounge. Behind that were two more passenger cabins. Finally, in the rear was the private suite Mrs. Roosevelt and Vicky would occupy. It was in fact an even more luxurious cabin, with its own dressing room, outfitted so it could be converted into a bridal suite.

"Besides yourselves, we are carrying forty passengers," the captain said. "We can carry more, but when we convert the cabins for sleeping at night, we have just forty berths. Besides myself, only one steward and one stewardess know who you are. One of them will answer your bell. No one else. Latch your door after I leave, and if you don't admit anyone but my two people, no one should discover who's aboard. The weather over the Atlantic looks good. We should have a smooth flight and land at Lisbon at four o'clock tomorrow afternoon. If there is anything *I* can do for you, let me know."

The Secret Service agents had followed through the airplane, bringing the luggage. When it was in place, Vicky latched the door.

"Privacy," she said. From her mouth it came out "pvrr-ee-vatsy."

"Good," said Mrs. Roosevelt. "I am going to get rid of these grotesque clothes and dress in my own fashion."

During recent years the necessity of meeting a tight schedule had brought the First Lady more and more often aboard airplanes. She had never, even so, rid herself of a sense that making a trip by air was adventuresome and something of a sacrifice. As recently as April 15 she had written in her newspaper column that flying from Washington to Los Angeles for Jimmy's wedding had been "very strenuous." This flight was different.

The flight had only four interesting events: two takeoffs and two landings. For a minute or so during the first takeoff, the airplane seemed likely to shake itself to pieces before it could manage to lift its great weight from the water. The engines screamed out a deafening roar, and the Clipper at first wallowed in the waves, then charged into them and hit each one with ever-increasing violence, until the loud slap-slap of hull against water was deafening. It got worse and worse . . . and then abruptly it ceased, as the flying boat lifted away from the water and rose majestically into the air.

The windows in the Clipper were not portholes but real windows of generous size, and the First Lady and Vicky had a fine view of New York as the airplane climbed and turned out over the Atlantic.

Mrs. Roosevelt changed her clothes. Vicky changed hers— into a light gray maid's uniform with cap and apron.

A European, Vicky accepted every drink that was offered by the steward: *schnapps*, as she called it, meaning a whiskey before lunch, then wine with lunch and a brandy after, then two more whiskeys during the afternoon, an aperitif before dinner, a bottle of wine with dinner, and a liqueur after, followed by a brandy offered when the beds were turned down. It didn't affect her much. The First Lady accepted only a sherry before dinner and one glass each of the lunch and dinner wines.

"Americans," Vicky laughed over dinner, "know *nichts* of food and drink. Prohibition you had. How philistine!"

They flew east, over broken clouds at first, affording them a view of the sea and the shipping lanes. Then cloud obscured the ocean, and they could see nothing but the tops of clouds: fascinating at first but soon boring. They dozed part of what was the afternoon at home, because they'd been up so early, and when they were fully awake again the sun had set.

When the steward had left for the last time, Vicky took off her clothes. All her clothes. Mrs. Roosevelt hurried to pull the curtains over the windows at each side of the cabin. Vicky laughed. Who could see? she asked. Then she slept nude. Mrs. Roosevelt donned her nightgown, robe, and slippers before she sat down in the dressing room to pin up her hair. Vicky was snoring by the time the First Lady returned to the cabin. Looking at the sleeping girl, only half covered by one of the sheets, Mrs. Roosevelt wondered which of them had styled her life better. Was it a European attitude, more sophisticated? Or the new generation? She wondered if her daughters-in-law slept nude.

Landing was interesting. The Azores, their refuelling stop, lay under an overcast. The Clipper descended gradually and entered the clouds. Mrs. Roosevelt had heard of blind flying, but this was the first time she had ever experienced it; on past flights, if the destination airport could not be seen from above, the pilot did not land there. She realized this pilot had no choice; the airplane could not carry enough fuel to reach Lisbon nonstop. She wondered what he would have done if he'd had a choice. Perhaps nothing different, for after ten minutes or so of flying inside cloud, which was like being in a thick fog, the airplane emerged beneath the clouds. The ocean and the islands were in sight.

Lisbon lay under a bright afternoon sun. They had a view of the city. The Clipper landed in the upper harbor, a little up the river, actually, and wallowed like an awkward boat to a floating pier not unlike the one in New York.

Mrs. Roosevelt and Vicky remained in their suite in the rear of the Clipper until after sunset. They closed their curtains and had one more meal. Mrs. Roosevelt dressed in one of her khaki-twill out-fits. In her underwear, Vicky strapped the shoulder holster under her arm and settled her pistol into it. Then she dressed in khaki, too, in a sort of military uniform which, to Mrs. Roosevelt's sur-prise, consisted of a mannish-looking shirt and a pair of oversized trousers cinched tight around her waist by a leather belt.

Someone knocked on the door of the suite.

"Who is it?"

"Colonel Donovan's friend," said a man's voice.

Vicky stood back with her hand inside her shirt and on her pistol, while the First Lady opened the door.

"Kevin O'Neil's the name," said the man, speaking in a rich Irish accent. "I'm your guide and guard for Vichy France."

O'Neil was a man of about forty, as Mrs. Roosevelt judged. He was tall and robust, with a long face, pale blue eyes, and a toothy smile. He wore a somewhat soiled and wrinkled belted raincoat and a tweed hat.

"I've no credentials, so ye'll have to trust me for a bit. Any-way—*Je regrette de vous faire attendre. Es tut mir leid, Sie warten zu lassen.* Both languages, you see. Is my German too badly accented, Miss Klein?"

"You sound Bavarian," she said wryly.

"You sound Irish," said Mrs. Roosevelt. "That's how you sound, even in French."

"I wonder why? But it will be an asset, if ye don't mind my sayin' so. Knowin' the Irish disaffection for the English, the Ger-mans assume Irish neutrality bends toward them. I get a cordial welcome in their part of the world."

"What do you do, Mr. O'Neil?" asked Vicky.

"Meself? Well, I'll have to explain that as time allows. Right now, our carriage awaits. May I help with your luggage?"

His "carriage" was a small motor launch drawn up beside the Clipper on the side opposite the dock. He lowered their luggage into the boat and helped the two women aboard. Keeping his throttle out and the engine only gurgling, he guided the launch away from the Clipper in the shadow of its wing and quietly slipped away into the waters of Lisbon's harbor.

"I hope ye're not susceptible to seasickness," he said. "We've some distance to travel."

They did indeed: more than twenty miles, and it took more than two hours. Running slowly and quietly, he guided the launch down the harbor toward the sea, threading among the ships moving in and out. They passed by the lighted city of Lisbon on the right—gleaming when most cities of Europe were blacked out. The lights of moving cars flashed across the water. Mrs. Roosevelt spotted a lighted Ferris wheel turning in a waterfront park.

O'Neil pointed at a ship lying at anchor. It was lighted, and the sounds of music and laughter echoed over the water. *"Kaiserin Augusta,"* he said. "Rest and recreation for U-boat officers. A floating dance hall and bordello. Month after month. The officers come after long tours of duty, some from as far away as Canadian waters, to enjoy what a neutral port can afford."

"Where are the U-boats?" asked Vicky.

"You'll see them," said O'Neil.

As they neared the harbor entrance, he pushed in his throttle to give the launch power to overcome the current of an incoming tide. The boat bucked over the surging waves above the bar, and shortly they were on the open Atlantic, though still close to the Portuguese shore.

O'Neil pointed at some distant lights. "Casinos," he said. "Estoril. The Portuguese Riviera. If you can afford to live there, you can forget there's a war. But— Look at the low black shadow between us and the beach. See it? You wanted to see a U-boat? That's one. And there will be four or five others around, lying dark on the surface. I hope I don't ram one."

Mrs. Roosevelt noticed that O'Neil was navigating carefully. He had a compass with a set of sights on top, and from time to time he took fixes on landmarks ashore, then adjusted his course. He cut his power again, and the launch slowed. It wallowed in the waves, and induced a little nausea in the First Lady, who would have preferred to keep moving against the surge.

O'Neil used his compass to determine a direction out at sea. When he was satisfied, he pulled a large flashlight from under the launch's wheel and flashed a signal. He waited a minute, then did it again. He cut the engine entirely, and they waited, the boat rising and falling and rocking.

"Ah. There we have it," he muttered.

Fifty yards ahead the sea rumbled. A guttural roar followed. Then the surface erupted, and suddenly a massive dark shape rose and seemed to fill the horizon from north to south.

"Skipjack?" asked Mrs. Roosevelt hoarsely.

"God, let us hope so," said O'Neil. "She's no U-boat. There's none as big as that. No. That's an American fleet submarine. It's *Skipjack*, too, since she surfaced at my signal. *Skipjack*. Our luxury liner to the south of France."

As soon as they were aboard and a man from the submarine pulled away in the launch, the *Skipjack* got underway. Mrs. Roosevelt and Vicky were helped to climb to the bridge, where they were met by the skipper of the submarine, a surprisingly young man, Lieutenant Commander Richard Deakin.

"I'm honored to have you aboard, Mrs. Roosevelt," he said. "And Miss Klein. I'm afraid a submarine is not a very comfortable vessel, but we'll do our best to make it as little uncomfortable for you as possible."

"Thank you, Commander," said the First Lady. "We in turn will try to be as little trouble as possible."

He pointed to a round hole in the floor of the bridge. "Ma'am," he said. "That's the hatch. The officer below will help you on the ladder."

They descended into the conning tower of the submarine, a constricted chamber crammed with instruments and gauges and machinery. Kevin O'Neil followed, and then the officers came down from the bridge.

Lieutenant Commander Deakin spoke to Mrs. Roosevelt. "We're going to dive," he said. "It's perfectly safe. We're not going deep."

The First Lady nodded. She was apprehensive, but the President and Donovan had assured her that *Skipjack* was a new boat with an old crew. It would be a tame experience, they said. Good for them.

"Dive!" said the skipper.

One of the men pushed a big red button, and a raucous horn sounded. The deck slanted forward as the diving planes dragged the bow down and the submarine plunged beneath the ocean swell. The dive made all kinds of unnerving noises: hisses, churning, bubbling, creaking. It was accompanied, too, by a crisp, curt exchange of orders and responses among the officers and sailors manning the various stations in the conning tower.

Shortly the boat levelled off and became quieter.

"One hundred feet," said the skipper.

Mrs. Roosevelt had wondered if she would suffer an oppressive claustrophobia when she found herself in a submerged submarine. For a brief moment she labored for breath, until she realized that there was plenty of air to breathe and that none of the crew were gasping.

It was Vicky, in fact, who seemed to find submerging difficult. She was pale, and sweat glistened on her face. Kevin O'Neil noticed and regarded her with a subdued smile.

The submarine was no luxury liner. Lieutenant Commander Deakin gave the First Lady and Vicky his own cabin, the only private cabin aboard. It was a tiny space, with a bunk, a desk, a safe, a locker, and not enough room for the two women to sleep at the same time. They would have to sleep in shifts. They would have to spend most of their time in the wardroom or in the mess, since there really was no room for extra people in the conning tower. Deakin recommended they leave their luggage closed as much as possible, since everything inside a submarine sooner or later acquired a coating of oil.

There was, of course, no concealing from the crew that the tall woman who had come aboard at Lisbon was Mrs. Franklin D. Roosevelt. It may have been a breach of security, but she wrote her name on anything a crewman presented to her: hat, shirt, dollar bill, whatever.

Lieutenant Commander Deakin explained their course. They would run submerged until they were twenty miles or so off the Portuguese coast. Then they would run south on the surface for whatever remained of the night. That should bring them close to Cape St. Vincent, the southwesternmost point of Portugal. As daylight came, they would submerge. Tomorrow would be Friday, the 13th; and they would run all day submerged, making about nine knots. After sunset they would surface and rendezvous with a British destroyer who would escort them through the Strait of Gibraltar.

"After that," said Deakin, "we will run on the surface at night—assuming the lookouts spot nothing—and submerged during the day. We are looking to make a rendezvous on the French coast a little before dawn on Tuesday."

Eighty men lived in the jammed space of the submarine, but Mrs. Roosevelt found their morale surprisingly good—and concluded it was not a show for her, either. The boat was air-conditioned, so temperatures were comfortable. The air became heavy and unpleasant after a long run submerged, but when the boat surfaced it was somehow immediately filled with fresh air and the smell of the open sea.

The food was good. Mrs. Roosevelt made a point of eating in the crew's mess several times, and she learned that the pantry was open twenty-four hours a day. The crew could have coffee and doughnuts any time of day or night. Sandwiches were available almost any time. The regular meals were tasty and nutritious. There was little distinction between the crew's mess and the officers' mess—and the crew knew it.

Sitting in the wardroom while Vicky was asleep in the captain's cabin, Mrs. Roosevelt noticed Kevin O'Neil going into the cabin.

"Got a problem there," said Lieutenant Commander Deakin. "He's going in to share with her a nip of Irish whiskey. I told him drinking wasn't permitted on the boat, and he reminded me he is a neutral civilian and said he's not subject to my orders. I didn't argue with him. I did tell him, though, that if I caught him giving whiskey to any member of my crew, I'd throw all his whiskey overboard."

"I have to place a lot of trust in those two people," said the First Lady. "I do wish they would not drink."

The skipper's youthful face spread in a broad smile. "He's an Irishman," he said. "He's independent as a hog on ice."

"Where are we, Commander?"

Deakin glanced at his watch. "We'll be surfacing shortly. Come with me to the conning tower. In a little while, I can show you where we are."

In the conning tower she watched the skipper give commands that were to her mysterious, but she had learned to have confidence in the young man. She felt the submarine break the surface. The boat flooded with fresh air. Lookouts climbed the ladder and emerged through the hatch onto the bridge. The skipper and two other officers followed. After two or three minutes, Deakin called down, and she climbed the ladder and joined him on the bridge.

"Spain," he said, pointing to the left; and, pointing to the right, "Tangier."

They were in the Strait of Gibraltar. The coasts on both sides were lighted as if the world were at peace; but the narrow strait was patrolled by British warships, and they were dark shadows to both sides.

Deakin pointed to a shadow ahead. "Destroyer. Our escort. We're following him."

It was eerie to be in this fabled stretch of water, where Europe and Africa were no more than fifteen miles apart, where

the British, clinging determinedly to their fortress just ahead and
to the left, effectively bottled the Italian and German fleets in the
Mediterranean, keeping them from entering the Atlantic.

The destroyer flashed a signal. Mrs. Roosevelt thought she
could read a few of the letters in Morse code but had to conclude
that either the signalman flashed too fast for her or that the code
was not Morse. A man on the bridge aimed his light at the stern of
the destroyer, and she could hear the clack-clack of the opening
and closing shutter as he returned the signal.

"They've detected twenty German long-range patrol bombers
coming in from Sardinia," said Lieutenant Commander Deakin.

"Do we submerge?"

"They're a good twenty minutes away. They're not looking
for us, though. If they approach within five minutes' distance, we'll
dive."

A few minutes later they saw the German planes. Actually,
what they saw was streams of red fire going up toward them, from
half a dozen ships. They saw the sharp white flashes of exploding
anti-aircraft shells. They saw yellow fire in the air—one German
plane had been hit. They saw a red and yellow explosion on the
water—one British ship had been hit. A minute later the eastern
sky lit up with a confusion of streaking fire and explosions. Airplanes fell, trailing fire and smoke.

"RAF fighters," said the skipper. "I'd guess three German
bombers damaged or down, two fighters."

During the spectacle of the air attack, the destroyer and submarine had continued to move east at twenty knots. The destroyer
flashed another signal.

"He's breaking off," said Lieutenant Commander Deakin.
"We're in the Mediterranean now—and on our own."

Mrs. Roosevelt became accustomed to the routine aboard the submarine. They ran on the surface at night, making twenty knots,
and submerged at dawn. During the long daylight of summer they
kept submerged, making nine knots. Twice during one night the

watches spotted airplanes or a ship, and the boat dived fast. It was no cause for alarm, the skipper explained—just a precaution. No one but the British knew the *Skipjack* was in the Mediterranean. No one was looking for it.

After two days, the First Lady was bored—and was grateful for it. She divided her time between the skipper's cabin and the wardroom, with an occasional visit to the crew's mess. It was difficult to move around the boat without being in the way.

Vicky spent time playing cards with the officers and some of the crew, quickly learning and becoming skilled at a game they called acey-deucey. Kevin became even more skilled and won some money—which, however, he returned to the men he won it from, since he could not carry American money into Vichy France.

Mrs. Roosevelt would carry American money. There was no way she could deny her identity, and she had no intention of trying. If the secrecy of her mission were compromised, she would acknowledge who she was and say she had entered France from Spain, showing her passport to Spanish and French border guards, who waved her through without delay.

On June 17 the sun would rise on the southern coast of France at 4:34 A.M. The latest that the submarine should surface was 4:00 A.M. After that, the glow of approaching sunrise might silhouette it for a patrol boat.

By 3:45 Mrs. Roosevelt, Vicky, and Kevin O'Neil were in the conning tower, with their luggage. Lieutenant Commander Deakin held half of a set of earphones pressed to his ear and listened intently. His sound man was also listening. Deakin beckoned to Mrs. Roosevelt and offered her the earphones. She listened for a moment, distinctly hearing the sound of engines and a muttering sound she took for turning propellers.

"Fishing boats," said Deakin. "One of them is looking for us." Then he turned to one of the officers and said, "Periscope depth."

Shortly he raised the periscope and scanned the surface.

"Surface. Lookouts to the bridge."

She could feel the submarine's hull breaking the surface. Men scrambled up the ladder. A gush of water came down as the hatch was opened. They waited while the lookouts scanned the sea and sky. Then the skipper climbed the ladder. After another minute he called for the three civilians to come to the bridge.

Mrs. Roosevelt went up first. The morning was cool, gray-lighted. A fresh breeze had not yet whipped up any waves, and the submarine wallowed in gentle swells. Half a dozen boats lay around, shining bright lights on the water.

"That's how they attract fish to their nets," said Deakin. "Some fish are like moths, apparently."

One of the fishing boats approached the submarine.

"Here we come," said Deakin. "On time and good navigation."

The fishing boat was a small, rugged, working vessel, with a rude cabin amidships and decks covered with coiled nets. Its fishing light was not burning. It drew alongside. Crewmen threw ropes, which were caught by men on the deck of the submarine and looped around cleats.

Very carefully, yet very quickly, the First Lady and her companions, and their baggage, were transferred from the *Skipjack* to the fishing boat. As the boat moved slowly away, the submarine slipped silently beneath the swell. Mrs. Roosevelt regretted that she had not had time to thank Lieutenant Commander Deakin.

"*Je suis l'Huître,*" said the man at the wheel of the fishing boat. He was the OYSTER, which was his code name. He was a spare, late-middle-aged man with a grizzly gray-black beard. He said nothing more but spun the wheel and guided the boat toward the coast.

The sky in the east had begun to turn red when the fishing boat entered an inlet and approached a wharf in the middle of a village.

"*C'est Sète,*" said the OYSTER.

It was a fishing town. That the town depended on fishing was easy to see. The waterfront was lined with fish markets, already opening to receive the night's catch from scores of returning boats.

The OYSTER had held his speed down, and his boat was not the first to land. Policemen walked along the quay, but they saw no reason to take special interest in any particular boat.

The OYSTER pointed at two men who stood near the end of the quay. *"Boches,"* he spat. Germans.

A few small vans moved out onto the wharf. It was obvious what they would do; they would load with fish and shellfish, and ice, and rush for Paris, where the morning's catch would grace the table of some German officer tonight. One of the vans backed up to the OYSTER's boat. In an instant, Mrs. Roosevelt and her party transferred from the boat to the van. Then the OYSTER and the van driver mimicked vigorous haggling over the price of what the van would carry. Reaching a grudging agreement, the OYSTER and the driver carried boxes of fish from boat to van. Soon the First Lady and her friends shared the back of the smelly little vehicle with a load of fish.

The driver moved the van off the quay. He stopped at an ice house and himself shovelled ice into his boxes of fish.

Only when they were on the road out of town did he turn to his passengers and say, *"Je suis le Canard."* He was the DUCK.

He explained to them then that they must lie down among the boxes of iced fish and be covered with a tarpaulin. They would have to pass through several checkpoints, and only after that would it be safe for them to come out from under and sit up.

"It is necessary to remember," he said to them, "that many Frenchmen have become more Nazi than Hitler. It might be better to be questioned by a German officer than by a Vichy policeman."

IV

COULD THERE BE, BY definition, such a thing as a small and modest château? As compared to the great châteaux of the Loire Valley, Montrond was modest. Built on the upper reaches of the Loire, two kilometers from the village of Fleurs, in an area considered unfashionable by the builders of the great châteaux, Montrond dated from the fifteenth century. It was built by Roland Persigny, minister of war to King Louis XI, as a retreat far removed from the seats of power and had remained a property of the Counts of Persigny until 1819. In 1941 it was too far removed from Paris to be of any interest to the Germans and just far enough from Vichy to discourage the expenditure of scarce gasoline to drive to a château that was regarded as not only undistinguished, but nowhere.

Mrs. Roosevelt had been briefed about the château, its present owners and occupants, and so knew that—

It was in 1941 the property of a man named Lucien Lenclos, a wealthy vintner who had fled the country in 1940 and was living in Switzerland. His daughter, Vivienne Lenclos Duval, had remained in France because her husband had been taken prisoner near Sedan. She lived in the château and continued to try, by every means she could, to learn if her husband was alive, where he was, and when he might be returned to France. It was she who welcomed Mrs. Roosevelt to Montrond.

The château had been capriciously named, because it did not stand on a hill at all. To the contrary, the stones of its foundation were in the river itself, on its eastern side. Its foundation stones on the other three sides were in water, too—the water of the moat that had been dug around the château. In style, it was a small fortress that could be entered only by crossing the moat on a bridge that had once been a drawbridge. Four round towers, each in a different style, stood at the corners. Three of the towers had tall conical roofs. The fourth had a flat roof with embrasures from which, presumably, arrows could be shot at attackers.

All of this was formidable and unfriendly-looking. Inside the fortress stood a handsome home in a pleasant early-Renaissance style. A felicitous compromise had been reached between preserving the château and making it livable. The fortress exterior was used for storage, as a garage, and for the kitchen—which left much of it vacant. High rooms in the towers were used for guest rooms, though, and bathrooms had been installed. The ground between the fortress and the home was planted in formal gardens: hedges and flowers in geometric patterns.

The chief rooms were furnished with antiques, nothing more recent than the eighteenth century. The art that enriched those rooms would have been well worth the attention of German looters and might well have been taken away by now if the Germans had known it was there. Mrs. Roosevelt did not even try to appreciate it all at once but noted that the art varied from religious paintings by conspicuously devout artists to a bare-breasted portrait of the mistress of a seventeenth-century Count of Persigny. Tapestries of classical and religious scenes hung from the walls and must have glorified the rooms with vibrant color before they faded.

The First Lady and her party arrived at Montrond after a day and a half's drive from Sète. The driver had sold his load of fish to a restaurant-hotel at Avignon, after which he had driven away from the Rhone and followed country roads north through rugged country.

They were stopped twice at checkpoints, by Vichy police. No questions were asked of them, however, when the driver displayed a pass signed and stamped by the *Militärbefehlshaber im Frankreich*, the German Military Governor of France. So impressive was the rank and the stamps and seals on the document that they intimidated the police, who did not seem to think of questioning its validity. In any case, someone with fuel to drive a van had to be someone of official importance.

Madame Duval met the First Lady at the bridge. *"Bonjour, Madame,"* she said. *"Enchantée. Faites comme chez vous."*

Madame Vivienne Lenclos Duval, daughter of the owner of the château, was a woman of perhaps thirty years. She was beautiful, yet marked by endless damaging anxiety. The thinness of her blonde hair suggested illness—or maybe malnutrition, since she was thin to the point of emaciation. The bone structure of her face told her classic beauty, but her skin was stretched tight over it and was grayish in color. She made no tacit appeal for sympathy, yet Mrs. Roosevelt saw that she needed it and wanted it.

Mrs. Roosevelt had an instinct for this.

Madame Duval stood ahead of a small knot of servants. She gave her orders with quiet gestures, and the men and women moved to gather up luggage and carry it across the courtyard toward the house.

"Mademoiselle . . . ?" asked Vivienne Duval, nodding toward Vicky.

"Elle est ma fille de chambre," said Mrs. Roosevelt. *"Elle s'apppelle* Vicky."

Vivienne Duval gave orders that the lady's maid was to be housed conveniently near the lady.

"Et comment s'appelle ce monsieur?"

Mrs. Roosevelt was a bit surprised that her hostess did not know who would be accompanying her. *"Un Irlandais,"* she said. *"Un ami. Il s'appelle* Kevin O'Neil."

Madame Duval told her staff to house the Irishman in one of the tower suites.

"Now," she said, still speaking a French that Mrs. Roosevelt understood perfectly: the French of Mademoiselle Sylvestre at Allenswood so many years ago. "I should imagine you have not eaten well during this journey. Let us—including Monsieur O'Neil—meet on the terrace for lunch in half an hour."

The invitation had not included Vicky, the maid—as indeed Vicky had not expected it would. When Mrs. Roosevelt went down to lunch, Vicky, dressed now in a black dress with white apron and cap, busied herself unpacking the luggage and laying out Mrs. Roosevelt's things in her bathroom.

Kevin found that his tower suite consisted of a small sitting room, a small bedroom, and an oversized bathroom with a huge tub that could never be filled with the trickle of water that came from the tap. This was immaterial to him; he did not expect to stay long.

He turned back his bed to see if the bedclothes sheltered vermin. And there he found a note—

Sous le lit. Under the bed.

He checked there. Oho! A Schmeisser submachine gun. Now, who had put that there for him? He wouldn't touch it unless and until he needed. He burned the note in an ashtray.

Coming down to the terrace, Mrs. Roosevelt was startled to find a uniformed German officer, standing in a relaxed posture, chatting and sipping champagne with Vivienne Duval and Kevin O'Neil.

O'Neil had come to the terrace in wrinkled trousers, a tweed jacket that had seen better days, a white shirt in need of laundering, and a loosely knotted necktie.

"Allow me to introduce Colonel Artur Brandt," said Vivienne Duval. "He is one of the German delegates to your meeting."

The colonel put aside his glass, bowed stiffly, then extended his hand. "A great and memorable honor," he said in English.

Although Mrs. Roosevelt knew little about German uniforms

and insignia, she recognized the two silver lightning slashes on one of his black collar patches as the emblem of the SS. He was an unprepossessing figure, stocky and not nearly as tall as O'Neil. He was bald. What remained of his black hair had been clipped short around the sides. He wore small, round gold-rimmed eyeglasses, tightly affixed to his nose by thin gold temples that pinched his head. The lower frames pressed tiny furrows in his cheeks. His uniform was field gray, not the notorious black of the SS, but he wore breeches and black boots. Under the uniform jacket he wore a white shirt and a black necktie. He wore braided aluminum epaulets and a dress belt also of woven aluminum.

"It's to Colonel Brandt that we owe the excellent champagne," said Kevin O'Neil. "Six cases of it, I understand."

That brought a faint, quick smile to the face of the German officer. "I am pleased to be able to offer that small token of my esteem," he said.

Mrs. Roosevelt did not ordinarily care to drink wine at noon, but of course she accepted a glass of champagne. "It *is* excellent," she said.

"He has indeed brought six cases," said Vivienne Duval. Her accented and hesitant English demonstrated why she had spoken French to her American guest. "We are much . . . thanking."

The First Lady had been a shy girl and young woman but had long since overcome that and seldom found herself at a loss for words. She did now. Bill Donovan had not told her she would confront an SS officer at this meeting, and she wondered what was the significance of his presence.

"I can promise you the absolute security of this château for the duration of your visit," said the colonel.

"I assume, then, you are in charge of the security arrangements," said Mrs. Roosevelt.

The colonel nodded. "In a sense," he said. "The chief problem was to keep the Vichyites away from here. None of them are to be trusted. None of them. A man who would betray his own country would betray anyone else's country, just as readily. I told them an important man, from Berlin, was coming here for a meeting, so no one was to come near, no one was to see or hear anything."

"We are grateful," said Mrs. Roosevelt. "May I ask where you are stationed, Colonel?"

"In Vichy," he said. "Have you ever heard of an organization called *Sicherheitsdienst*? In English, Security Service. I am commander of the SD in Vichy France. My rank, actually, is not colonel but *Obersturmbannführer*, SS. It is the equivalent, roughly, of a lieutenant colonel—*Oberstleutnant* in the *Wehrmacht*."

She had not heard of the *Sicherheitsdienst*, but Donovan had warned her that the Gestapo operated openly in unoccupied France. German counterintelligence and counterespionage operations extended to the whole of France, not just to the occupied part. There might not be parades of *Wehrmacht* soldiers in the streets of cities like Vichy, Lyons, and Marseilles; but the German presence was heavily oppressive throughout the unoccupied zone.

"We are fortunate to have your cooperation, Colonel Brandt," said Mrs. Roosevelt.

"And you wonder why you have it," he said, showing another of his quick little smiles.

"I can't deny that I do wonder."

"The Führer has overreached himself and will, if he cannot be stopped, bring about the total defeat and destruction of Germany. I have always been a great admirer of Adolf Hitler. I have always been loyal to him, since I joined the Party in 1925. But I must give my first and greatest loyalty to my country."

"Do many members of the *Sicherheitsdienst* agree with you?"

"Very few," said Colonel Brandt. "*Very* few. But perhaps enough. A few in the SS, a few in the Gestapo. Many in the army. The *Wehrmacht*— Well . . . There can be no doubt that the Führer intends to invade Russia, probably this summer, probably within a few weeks. If he does that, we will be forced to fight again the two-front war that Bismarck dreaded. Bismarck, you will remember, was statesman enough to know that Germany will never be strong enough to fight the Russians in the east and the British or French in the west, at the same time."

"But it won't be a two-front war, now will it?" said Kevin O'Neil. "There is no front in the west. That ended at Dunkirk."

"Ah, but there is," said Brandt. "It's coming down on us from the air. We are fought at sea. And sooner or later the United States will join the British—as they have practically done now, with Lend-Lease, the declaration of an Atlantic security zone, and so on. While the German army is tied down in Russia, the British and the French and the Americans will move. My country will be defeated and destroyed. That is why I am dedicated to bringing the war to an end now, before Hitler invades Russia and makes our defeat inevitable."

"Will it be necessary to *kill* Hitler?" asked Kevin.

Obersturmbannführer Brandt sighed. "I should like to believe it could be avoided. I am afraid it cannot."

"Who will do it?"

"It will have to be someone he trusts. I may have to do it myself."

Their lunch was as excellent as was the champagne. The conversation was not as profound as had been that on the terrace. They could not open any important subject, said *Obersturmbannführer* Brandt, until General Rousseau and the other German representative arrived.

Mrs. Roosevelt concluded that the afternoon might be a good time to take a short nap. She accompanied Madame Duval on a tour of the château, admiring the art and appreciating the skills of the architects and builders, then went to her suite.

Vicky was there. She sat in a chair facing a window, looking out over the gardens, toward the wall of the outer fortifications of the château.

"Vicky. Is everything unpacked and in order?"

Vicky had insisted that the room might contain concealed microphones and that every word they spoke there should be as mistress to maid.

"Yes, Ma'am."

Vicky gestured that they should leave the suite. Mrs. Roosevelt accompanied her. They walked along a hall lined with paintings, none less than two hundred years old: most of them portraits of people the First Lady guessed even the owner of the château could not identify.

"Something has happened," said Vicky quietly.

"What?"

"On Friday the Vichy government arrested twelve thousand Jews. They will be shipped out of the country, probably to Poland."

Mrs. Roosevelt scowled. "Is there nothing we can do?"

"Who would do what?" Vicky asked bitterly. "What will the President do? Declare war against Germany?"

"Vicky—"

"I know. He can't. America doesn't care. At least, America doesn't care enough to make any kind of sacrifice. He can't even offer to take those twelve thousand into America. Oh, no! That would make far too many Jews in his holy Christian country!"

"The President does care, Vicky."

"I suppose so. I know *you* do. But it's the old, old story. No more Jews in America. They might want to join country clubs. No more Jews in Britain. They might appear with beards at the Derby. No more Jews in Palestine. That would offend the Arabs. None to Australia, none to New Zealand, none to Argentina or Brazil or Mexico! Some of these in France have fled Germany and Austria and Czechoslovakia. And here in France they are spies. Twelve thousand spies! I wish we had a tenth of that many!"

"What will happen to those people?" asked Mrs. Roosevelt.

"They will die," said Vicky. "Die. Some of disease. Some of malnutrition. Some of overwork. Some of abuse. And many will simply be murdered. After all, they are only Jews."

"I doubt that the President knows," said Mrs. Roosevelt.

"He knows," said Vicky. "Or soon will know. I transmitted the information."

"How did you find out?"

"One of the kitchen staff here is a Jew. Madame Duval doesn't know."

"Why did that person tell you?" asked Mrs. Roosevelt.

"She didn't. She only learned this morning that her mother and father were taken. She was crying. The household staff is sympathetic and all upset."

Mrs. Roosevelt shook her head sadly, "Vicky," she said, "if we succeed in what we are here to do, those people may be saved. They and other thousands. That's all I know to do."

"*Verdammte Nationalsozialistische Schweine!*" Vicky spat. "Do you know what they made me do? Crawl on the street in my underwear, scrubbing the sidewalk pavement with a brush. *Juden!* All the Jewish girls in my school. All of us! In our underwear! The crowd loved it! They kicked over our buckets, spilled our water, so we had to run back in the school and carry out more water. Half naked! They laughed. Oh, how they laughed!"

"How old were you, Vicky?"

"Eighteen. When things like that matter most. Worse things were to happen later."

"What can I say? Except to express my deepest sympathy."

Vicky drew a deep breath, stiffened her body, and seemed to struggle for self-control. "There is something you can do for me," she said.

"What?"

"Jews are not the only thing the Germans are shipping out of France. They are looting the country of food. Special rations have been arranged for this meeting, through the black market—so you will probably eat well. The household staff is malnourished. And I will be, too, if I have to eat nothing but what they get. Lunch was a plate of beans, with two thin slices of sausage."

"I'll have food brought up to this room," said Mrs. Roosevelt grimly.

* * *

When the First Lady woke from her nap, Vicky was there to tell her that two big cars had arrived, bringing General Paul Rousseau from Paris and a German officer whose name she had not been able yet to discover. Madame Duval had sent up word that the dinner party would gather on the terrace at seven.

That left time for a bath. Vicky attended, as if she had really been a maid.

"We can talk in these rooms," she said. "I've spent some time checking for microphones. I'm satisfied there are none."

"If you are satisfied, I am satisfied."

"I had a response to my report," Vicky said as she poured an herbal scent into the bath water where Mrs. Roosevelt soaked.

"What did they say?"

"They told me they already knew about the twelve thousand and asked me not to use our transmitter to send news of the world. I suppose it *was* a mistake. I used half a minute to send it. In that amount of time the Germans could possibly have achieved a fix on the signal. I suppose I was too emotional."

"You have every reason and every right to be emotional," said Mrs. Roosevelt. "You see, I know something of your family history. Colonel Donovan gave me the information."

"I doubt that Colonel Donovan knows it all," said Vicky resentfully.

"What he does know and told me is enough to give you every right to be emotional."

"Thank you. I'm sorry. I should understand that you are sympathetic."

Mrs. Roosevelt dressed for dinner, in an ankle-length ivory-colored silk gown with a lace bodice. She wore a simple string of pearls and a pearl bracelet.

Vivienne Duval wore black: an exquisite, form-fitting dress, knee length, with a diamond necklace and a diamond-and-emerald pin.

Kevin O'Neil appeared in a tweed suit, plus the same frayed shirt and necktie he had worn at noon.

Obersturmbannführer Brandt wore the uniform he had worn all day.

When Mrs. Roosevelt arrived on the terrace, General Paul Rousseau was already there. He wore the blue dress uniform of the French army. The eldest person there, he was gray and tired-looking. His face was dominated by a bushy white mustache. His eyes were surrounded by deep wrinkles, and his mouth seemed extended at both ends by two downward-curving creases.

If he was a tragic, defeated figure, he carried his consolation with him. An attractive young woman, taller than he was, clung to his arm.

"I will acknowledge that I am astonished that you have made so dangerous a journey, but I am most gratified that you are here," the general said to Mrs. Roosevelt when they were introduced. "Allow me to present Mademoiselle Gabrielle. She is a fashion model, with Schiaparelli."

He gave no further name for the young woman. She was Gabrielle, which was apparently all the name she had. Her hair was wrapped in a black turban. She wore a black knit dress under a white single-breasted jacket fastened with three large white and gold buttons. Her skirt was fashionably short, skirts above the knee being in fashion in a Europe where fabrics were in short supply. She wore black gloves. Her eyes were narrow, beneath heavy dark eyebrows, and her lips were heavily reddened with lipstick.

Gabrielle apparently had little to say. She murmured in French that she was pleased to meet Mrs. Roosevelt and then fell silent and resumed fawning over the general.

"We are concerned," said General Rousseau, "about the British representative. Mr. Randolph Churchill should be here, but he has not arrived. We can hardly open serious discussions without a representative of the British government."

"Allow me to assure you the British representative will arrive yet this evening, *Monsieur le Général,*" said *Obersturmbann-führer* Brandt in English.

"And the representative of the *Wehrmacht?*" asked General Rousseau.

"Is here," said Brandt. "For the sake of secrecy, he had himself flown here in a small and spartan military aircraft. He is resting and bathing but will be with us momentarily."

"I hope he is a man who can speak for the army," said General Rousseau.

"You will be assured on that point when you meet him," said the *Obersturmbannführer*. "But let me make a point. That *he* is here is the greatest secret of this meeting. He has the most to lose. I am already concerned that too many people will know."

"The only person you didn't expect is Gabrielle," said the general. "I am trusting my own life to her discretion. Your general can entrust his."

The identity of the representative of the *Wehrmacht* was a complete surprise. He was not the man expected by Donovan or by the President.

He was stocky, of a little more than average height, dressed in field gray, with long trousers, not breeches and boots—and the trouser legs were adorned with two broad scarlet stripes, insignia of his very high rank. He wore two medals at his throat: one an exceptionally large Iron Cross, the other a more elaborate combination of cross, star, and leaves fashioned from gold and blue enamel. Mrs. Roosevelt knew what that was; it was the fabled *Pour le Mérite*, the Blue Max, awarded sparingly by the Kaiser to the greatest military heroes of imperial Germany and not awarded since 1918.

Brandt introduced the general to Mrs. Roosevelt first. "Madame, I have the honor to present General Erwin Rommel."

The Desert Fox! He was deeply tanned from the North African sun. His lips were split from too-long exposure to that sun. His eyes seemed to be still squinting into a sunlit desert. His forehead was high, his cheekbones prominent, his mouth thin and tight.

He bowed and seemed to expect her to offer her hand to be kissed. When she didn't, he reached for her right hand and clasped it for a moment. The moment was awkward, for obviously he didn't speak or understand English. *"Je suis enchanté,"* he said. His French was not good either, but she could understand it.

"I am surprised you can be spared from your duties, General Rommel," she said in French. "I am even more surprised that you can get away without your absence being noticed."

The Rommel smile was tight and restrained. "In Tunis they think I am in Tripoli. In Tripoli they think I am in Tunis. In Berlin they think I am at Benghazi. But I can't stay away long. Apart from the secret, I cannot leave my army for long."

General Rousseau saluted Rommel, then extended his hand, and the two soldiers shook hands in what appeared to be genuine respect for each other. General Rousseau introduced Gabrielle, who was conspicuously impressed by the German general.

"Our charming hostess," said Brandt, presenting Vivienne Duval. "And finally, Monsieur Kevin O'Neil. An Irish soldier of fortune, I believe would be his description. And I believe his further description might be that he is Mrs. Roosevelt's personal bodyguard."

Kevin shook Rommel's hand, showing him a lazy smile. Mrs. Roosevelt noticed and was a little amused by the contrast between the military carriage of the German and the indolent posture of the Irishman. Kevin spoke French and said he was always pleased to meet a man who was the best at whatever he did—"Whether that be leading and army or cracking a safe."

Rommel was stiff but he was amused. "I know you don't lead an army, Monsieur O'Neil," he said, "but should I assume then that you crack safes?"

"Yes, but I'm not good at it," said Kevin.

Rommel laughed.

*　*　*

When they went in to dinner, Randolph Churchill still had not arrived. General Rousseau insisted they could not really negotiate anything in the absence of the British representative, so the conversation was mostly inconsequential.

Rommel did explain himself, in much the same terms that Brandt had used at noon: that he deeply feared Hitler was about to bring a fatal catastrophe on Germany by invading the Soviet Union.

"Speaking informally, General Rommel," said Mrs. Roosevelt, "what sort of peace do you foresee? What will Germany expect to retain of its conquests?"

Rommel shrugged. "I would assume we will withdraw our forces from France, Belgium, Luxembourg, the Netherlands, Denmark, and Norway, restoring those countries to their own governments. We will, however, wish to retain those parts of Poland that were German in 1914—which were most unjustly taken from us at Versailles. The *Anschluss*—that is to say, the union of the two great German-speaking countries, Germany and Austria—is permanent. Similarly, the Sudetenland, which is populated by Germans, must remain ours and not returned to Czechoslovakia." He shrugged again. "I assume we will want some such terms as those."

"What about Alsace-Lorraine?" asked General Rousseau.

"Bargaining chip," said Rommel. "Personally, I would return those provinces to France—provided, of course, that France agrees to our other claims."

"What of the Jews?" asked Mrs. Roosevelt.

Rommel nodded at Brandt. "I think *Obersturmbannführer* Brandt should speak to that."

Brandt frowned. "We are in the process of expelling the Jews from Germany, resettling them in Poland. We are building homes for them there. Horror stories about their abuse are simply untrue. They are propaganda. Of course, mistakes have been made, but— On the whole, the Jews are well treated. Poland may not be the right place for them. They would rather go to Palestine. With the cooperation of Britain and France, the two nations that control the Middle East, we can arrange resettlement of millions of Jews there. The Führer has suggested they should be given the island of Madagascar as a homeland. The point is, the Jews are a nation and should have a homeland of their own, instead of living in ours."

"General, do you agree?" Mrs. Roosevelt asked Rommel.

"I know little of this," said Rommel. "It is a political question."

"What about the French Jews?" asked General Rousseau. "Are they to be resettled in the new Jewish homeland?"

"The government of unoccupied France has indicated that is its wish," said Brandt. Then he smiled and added, "The government of unoccupied France will agree to anything we suggest."

"A restored French government might not agree to any such thing," said General Rousseau.

"No very great problem, I should think," said Rommel. "We won't tell you what to do with your Jews, and you won't tell us what to do with ours."

Brandt left the table twice and returned each time to say he could not discover why Randolph Churchill was delayed. The expected hard negotiating could not begin that evening. Conceding that, the company around the dinner table relaxed a measure.

Everyone drank—Kevin O'Neil in particular, but he was joined by General Rousseau and Gabrielle. Rommel drank as much as anyone, but it did not loosen him. He sat and watched, sipping wine, then brandy, and observing with his narrow eyes, his taut smile well under control.

Brandt leaned over and spoke to Mrs. Roosevelt in confidence. "A friend of yours wishes to come and visit you here. I have granted permission. She will probably arrive tomorrow."

"Whoever it is, Colonel, we seem to be confiding in far too many people."

"I do not believe you would want me to deny this woman the chance to speak with you."

"Who is it, Colonel?"

"You will be paid a visit by Miss Gertrude Stein. I believe she will be accompanied by her friend Alice B. Toklas."

Lying in bed waiting for sleep, Mrs. Roosevelt appraised what she had experienced so far. She had always been faintly skeptical of the demand that *she* be the American representative to this meeting, skeptical of the rationalization that the presence of the President's wife and of the Prime Minister's son would demonstrate good faith. She wondered now if the rationalization had not proved true. That the chief German representative should be General Rommel demonstrated something, surely, and good faith was likely what.

She had never heard of Colonel Artur Brandt, of course, and his presence was not impressive.

But General Rommel! The Desert Fox! Taking time away from his heavy responsibilities in North Africa to come here to discuss removing Hitler from office and arranging a negotiated peace! If the *Wehrmacht* really meant to act independently of Hitler, it could hardly have chosen a more eminent representative.

She did not know the details of Rommel's history. He had commanded a Panzer division in the Blitzkrieg of 1940, as she recalled. She seemed to recall she had heard his name in connection with the invasion of Poland. Unless she was wrong, he had been for a time a member of Hitler's personal staff. That he should have turned against his Führer was hardly believable.

Yet— He wore the *Pour le Mérite*, the highest honor the old imperial Germany could bestow on an officer. That meant he had served with great distinction in the last war. It might also mean he was committed to the traditions of the aristocratic officer corps. It might even mean that for years he had concealed his contempt for his Führer and the men around him.

Brandt . . . Why was he bringing Gertrude Stein here? Obviously—it *was* obvious, wasn't it?—she could not have known about this meeting unless he told her. If that was not the fact, then the word had gone much, much too far.

With her thoughts fastened on that question, Mrs. Roosevelt felt sleep overcoming her.

Then— A knock on the door.

"Qui est là?"

"Vicky."

"Come in."

Vicky shoved the door open and rushed in, closing and latching the door behind her. "Something awful has happened," she whispered hoarsely.

Mrs. Roosevelt subdued the offense she took at the way Vicky expressed herself. "What do you mean?"

"Brandt is dead."

"How?"

"Somebody put a slug through the back of his head."

THAT COLONEL ARTUR BRANDT had been murdered was beyond doubt. No man could shoot himself in the back of the head. The body lay face down. The entry wound was small. Mrs. Roosevelt dreaded the sight of the exit wound.

"Well . . ." said Kevin O'Neil. "I suppose it's possible. Shootin' yerself in the back of the head, that is. If a man were sufficiently determined— But, no. If he'd done that, the weapon would be lyin' nearby. We have to believe the man was murdered by person or persons unknown. And it does create for us something of a problem, I do believe."

"Enough of a problem to transmit 2391 ? ?" Vicky asked.

"No. No, I think not yet," said Kevin. "Unless, that is, the madame wishes to leave."

Mrs. Roosevelt shook her head. "Not for the moment. We have to think this thing through. With a man like General Rommel here to talk about a negotiated peace, we cannot simply flee because— Too much is at stake for us to run."

"We may have to," said Vicky. "After all—"

"We may very well," said Mrs. Roosevelt. "But not this moment, not this hour. Who killed him?"

Kevin O'Neil grinned broadly. "The pregnant question," he chuckled. "If we knew that, we'd know a whole lot."

"More important for the moment," said Mrs. Roosevelt, "is the question, how many people know he's dead?"

"I can answer that, I think," said Vicky. "So far, just one person besides us. He had called the kitchen and asked for a bottle of cognac. Before it could be delivered, he was killed."

"How did he call?" asked Mrs. Roosevelt. "There is no telephone in *my* room."

Vicky pointed at the wall. "Speaking tube," she said. "There is one of those in your room."

The young woman was right. Mrs. Roosevelt had seen old-fashioned speaking tubes in many houses: in fact, in the houses where she had grown up as a girl. As a child she and her cousins had played with them, going to the kitchen and calling to each other through the walls. The memories flooded back.

Just inside the mouthpiece on the wall was a small plate with a tiny hole in it. That was the whistle. When you wanted to call, you used a little lever to close the whistle plate over the mouthpiece, and you blew. The whistle would sound distinctly in the servants' station downstairs. A servant would inquire what you wanted, and you could call through the tube. If you spoke loudly and distinctly, your orders would be heard.

All this had long since been replaced by wired bells and even telephones. But not in the Château Montrond.

"He called through the tube," said Vicky. "A maid picked up a bottle of cognac, put it on a tray with a glass, and hurried up here. Between the time when he called and the time when she arrived, he was shot to death. Say three or four minutes."

"Where is the maid?" asked Mrs. Roosevelt.

"She has gone back downstairs. She promised me she would tell no one what she had found when she came into the room."

"But why did she tell *you?* How did you find out Colonel Brandt was dead?"

"The maid," said Vicky, "is the girl whose parents were taken in Friday's roundup of Jews. She doesn't know exactly who I am, but she knows I am sympathetic to the plight of the Jews—and assumes you are—and brought this news directly to me. She is terrified. She says that when the Gestapo arrives to investigate the death of Brandt, they will arrest and torture her."

"Maybe *she* killed him," said Kevin. "She had motive enough."

"If she didn't," said Mrs. Roosevelt, "then there are two people besides her and the three of us who know that Colonel Brandt is dead."

"Of course," said Kevin. "We three, the maid, and the murderer."

Mrs. Roosevelt stared for a moment at the body. "When word of this death reaches the two generals, the conference is over," she said. "We'll have come here for nothing. The hopes we placed in the meeting are dead."

"Surely you are not suggesting we could conceal—?"

Mrs. Roosevelt nodded at Vicky. "Not for very long, I suppose. But maybe long enough. Maybe through noon tomorrow will be long enough. If we can only get General Rousseau and General Rommel together long enough to reach even the outlines of an agreement, that may be all we need."

"We'll have to hide the body," said Kevin. "How in the world—?"

"Not impossible in a place like this," said Mrs. Roosevelt. "There must be a hundred rooms in this château, and I would guess that twenty of them at the very least are never used."

Kevin frowned. "Maybe we could weight him down and dump him in the river."

"Without anyone seeing?" asked Vicky.

"The place is dark as the pits of hell," said Kevin. "They've got no electricity to waste and are burnin' almost no lights."

"The maid who found the body . . ." said Mrs. Roosevelt. "She must know the premises. We need to talk to her anyway. Where is she, Vicky?"

"In the kitchen, I think. I asked her to wait there."

"Would you go get her, please?"

* * *

The young woman's name was Jeanine Charlet, and Mrs. Roosevelt guessed she was not as old as she looked. She was short, broad-hipped, and busty; and the First Lady conjectured that she had been a plump and jolly girl until she began to live daily with dread and hunger.

They spoke French, and Mrs. Roosevelt quickly explained to Jeanine Charlet what she wanted to do: to conceal the murder and the body for as long as possible.

"Jeanine," said Vicky. "We cannot promise you anything. Not anything at all. But I imagine you have some idea who the two generals are, and maybe you have some idea why they are here. If they succeed in what they are trying to do, that might—only might, not for sure—save your father and mother and the other people seized last Friday."

Jeanine nodded. "I will do anything I can."

"If he is not to be found, we must hide him," said Kevin. "Where can we put him? I suggested weighting him down and throwing him in the river."

Jeanine stared at the corpse. "And the rug is stained with blood," she said. "You must hide that, too. Plus, there is one more problem. He drove his own car here. It is parked on the other side of the bridge. So long as that car is there, it will be supposed he is here."

"This gets more and more complicated," said Vicky.

"Too much is at stake for us to allow ourselves to be intimidated," said Mrs. Roosevelt. "I have several times assisted the authorities in solving a murder mystery. I have never before tried to hide a body and prevent the discovery of a murderer."

"We have to find out who did it," said Kevin. "I mean, suppose he was killed by the Gestapo, who know why he's here."

"A place to hide the body," said Jeanine. "There is an old well, dug very deep and lined with stone, in the days when the owner of this château must have thought he might be besieged here. There is water in the bottom: slimy and dirty water that no one would think of trying to drink. Wrap him in the rug. Tie on some weights. Drop him down there. He might be down there for years before anyone found him. He might never be found."

"You must help us," said Kevin. "To find the place, to find rope and the weights."

"Yes. And find a way to carry him out so no one sees us. I know how."

"Then what about the car?" Vicky asked. "What are we going to do with that?"

"I know where to take it," said Jeanine. "Friends of mine. They will hide it. We must find the keys."

Kevin knelt beside the body of *Obersturmbannführer* Brandt and began to go through the pockets. "Can you drive?" he asked Jeanine.

"No. Vicky must drive."

"I will drive," said Kevin.

"Vicky must drive," said Jeanine. "The police are accustomed to seeing girls coming to the château early in the morning, dressed in maids' uniforms. We will have to walk. Do any of you have papers for this area?"

Vicky shook her head. "We have no papers but our passports."

Jeanine shrugged. "We will walk across the fields," she said. "Barefoot, so as not to muddy our shoes. If they see us, they'll take us for two maids walking to work. They won't come out in the mud to check us."

"Here are the keys," said Kevin. "I guess we've got a job of work cut out for us."

"Return here when you have disposed of the body," said Mrs. Roosevelt. "I want to go through the colonel's things. We may find some interesting information in his papers."

Vicky wrapped Brandt's head in a big bath towel, so blood would not drip as Kevin carried the body from the room and down the stairs. Jeanine rolled up the bloodstained rug. Vicky, with her pistol drawn, led the way into the hallway.

It was all but dark, and for a minute or so the three—Kevin, Vicky, and Jeanine—stood in the hallway, letting their eyes adjust to the darkness and listening intently for any sound.

No sound came from Rommel's room. From General Rousseau's they heard a grunt, then a high-pitched laugh, muffled by the heavy wooden door.

Vicky started down the stairs, down first to a landing, then down a longer flight to the ground floor. She hurried ahead and opened a door to the center courtyard of the château.

The night was chilly and damp. The moon shone above a thin overcast. A little of its light came through, but not much. In the darkness, Kevin stumbled over a sculpted low hedge and fell to his knees. The body dropped to the ground. The towel fell off, and Vicky rewrapped it. She walked just ahead of him after that, feeling her way along a walk of fine gravel.

They reached a door opening into the landward wing of the château. Now Jeanine led, since she knew her way through that wing and out to the rear grounds, where the old stables lay beneath the rear wall.

She reached the well. It was covered with a crude wooden lid, which she pulled aside. Immediately, without weighting it, she dropped the bloody rug. It seemed to fall for a long time before they heard the muted splash.

"Weight," Kevin whispered to her. "We've got to weight him down."

"I know how," said Jeanine.

She led him to the stone wall of the long stable, in the shadow of an overhanging roof. She pointed, and he could just make out a bundle of chains hanging from a beam. Traps. Heavy steel traps, suitable for bear or wolves. When he touched them he found them scaly with rust. She was right. A dozen of them would be heavy enough to sink the body. What was more, the rusty old clasps that had been used to secure the traps to trees could still be forced open and used to fasten the chains and traps to *Obersturmbann-führer* Brandt.

The clasps were stiff. Two of them resisted so much he gave up on them. In five minutes, even so, Kevin had ten or twelve of the old traps chained to the body.

He tipped the bulk of the corpse, with the rattling steel, over the stone edge of the well, and it all fell and crashed into the water below.

It was very different from anything Mrs. Roosevelt had ever done before—working to frustrate the police instead of cooperating fully with them. On the other hand, she had never tried to function before in a milieu where there was no access to justice, where there was no lawful authority to which she could appeal for help. American law officers, though sometimes stupid and occasionally venal, generally sought to enforce the law and to do justice. Here, no one in power was interested in doing right—as witness the arrest of twelve thousand Jews. All of those people, men, women, and children, were accused of being spies, enemies of the state. How could you treat honestly with a government like that? How could you rely on it to investigate a crime and attempt to bring the malefactor to justice?

She had never felt so alone, so remote from everyone committed to fairness and legality. The First Lady had never faced so grave a peril.

The chance that this wild, wild mission would achieve its purposes had never been good, and she had known that from the beginning. If, though, it should succeed, it would be worth any sacrifice she could make to it. Any sacrifice for her, any for Viktoria Neustadt, any for Kevin O'Neil. She wanted them to make their own commitments, and she was confident they had. They might none of them survive this week. If they did not, they would have died in an honorable cause.

As would have General Rousseau and General Rommel. They were here! The mission was not so rash after all.

She had returned to her room for gloves, so her fingerprints would not be on Brandt's possessions that she meant to examine. Fortunately, her room was only two rooms along the hall from his, and a pale moon shed enough light to leave the hall a little less than pitch dark.

She carried a small flashlight. They had left the room light on before, but now it seemed unwise to allow a light to show from the colonel's window. First, she made a general scan. In the wardrobe, Colonel Brandt had hung two uniforms and two civilian suits. One of the uniforms was the distinctive black suit worn by the SS, complete to the grinning death's-head on the cap. His shirts, neckties, socks, handkerchiefs, and underclothes were in the bureau, so neatly unpacked and arranged in the drawers that she wondered if he had done it himself or had ordered a maid to do it. Under his shirts lay a pistol: a 9mm Luger, plus one extra magazine of ammunition. His three suitcases were stacked in a corner.

It was all distinctly bourgeois. Except that two of the suits were uniforms, his clothes were the clothes of a small-town insurance agent or real-estate broker, chosen to make him presentable at church or at a meeting of the Rotary Club.

Documents. She had studied German at Allenswood; and, though not fluent in it, could read it, if somewhat laboriously.

Obersturmbannführer Brandt's credentials and orders lay among the papers in his briefcase.

His orders, three times countersigned and a dozen times stamped, constituted him *Höchst des Sicherheitsdienst im Sud Frankreich*—meaning Chief of the Security Service in South France: the unoccupied zone. The orders were signed *Heydrich, SS-Obergruppenführer.*

Reinhard Heydrich. The name was hardly known in the United States, but Bill Donovan had given his name to Mrs. Roosevelt as that of an SS general who was maybe the very most murderous of all the Nazis.

Also among Brandt's papers was his paybook: the bound document carried by all German soldiers, and apparently SS men as well, containing a detailed record of all their service. She laid it aside for later examination.

In the briefcase she found a file folder containing twenty or so sheets of typewritten paper. The typed language was formal and stilted and couched in a strange idiom she had never read before, but she gathered from as much of it as she could read that Colonel Brandt had received and digested a substantial quantity of reports indicating that Jews within his *Frankreich-Sud* jurisdiction were engaging in activities inimical to the security of the state. He had not signed an order for their arrest, but he had indicated to his Vichy counterpart that the *Sicherheitsdienst* expected French officials to do their duty to overcome subversion.

It meant that the SD, under the command of *Obersturmbannführer* Artur Brandt bore a heavy responsibility for the arrest of the twelve thousand French Jews, whose arrests could not imaginably be rationalized under any standard of law or justice.

In the drawer of a little antique desk, Mrs. Roosevelt found something else of special interest: a ceremonial dagger in a tooled leather scabbard. The colonel, it appeared, had not been confident he would return from the visit to the Château Montrond and had been carrying with him some of his keepsakes. Besides that, she found in the same drawer a small leather folder crammed with photographs.

She opened the folder and was viewing the first of the photographs when she heard a knock on the door.

"Qui est là?"

"Kevin," said O'Neil as he opened the door and walked in.

Mrs. Roosevelt switched off the little flashlight and left them almost invisible to each other in what little gray moonlight entered the room through the windows.

"The body?" she asked.

He made a swooping gesture. "Down the well. May I offer you a caution, dear lady?"

"Of course."

"Those two girls, Vicky and Jeanine, have full reason for hating the Nazis. Full reason. Couldn't have better reason. But beware of their emotions. Their passions could lead them to foolishness."

Mrs. Roosevelt could hardly see his face. "Let me ask you a question, Mr. O'Neil," she said.

"I will answer truthfully if I can," he said. "And untruthfully if I can't."

"Agreed," she said. "So tell me— Exactly why are *you* here? I can understand the two girls' motives. What are yours?"

"Ah, and there's a simple answer to that simple question," said Kevin. "Did Donovan not tell you? Typical Irishman! Sure. He didn't tell you. All right. I am here, Mrs. Roosevelt, because I am receivin' for this week's work—two weeks' work—ten thousand pounds, sterling. Rate of exchange? Well, the pound has fallen against the dollar. But I believe I can say I am receivin' somethin' like fifty thousand dollars, American. Motive. Motive enough? I am a mercenary."

"Do you care anything for the cause?" she asked.

"The British cause? Nothin'. The Germans could, with my blessin', defeat and occupy England, Wales, and Scotland . . . Except for one little thing. That little thing is that then they'd cross th' Irish Sea and occupy Ireland. And what's to stop them? Nothin'. I hate the Brits. But I hate the Krauts more. I've got good reason for the one—and equally good reason for the other."

"What about the arrest of the twelve thousand Jews?" she asked.

"I've got no great love for the Jews," he said. "But them as would kill—and kill is what we're talkin' about, are we not?— twelve thousand Jews would kill twelve thousand of any as offended them."

"Yes."

"Somehow . . . I'm not sure why I feel this. But somehow I'm dead certain *I* would offend them. It's for sure I'd *try*."

He couldn't see her smile in the darkness, but Mrs. Roosevelt smiled and nodded. "I think we can understand and trust each other, Mr. O'Neil," she said.

He moved toward her, a dark shadow but not menacing. Suddenly she found herself clasped affectionately in his arms. "We can work together, and we will," he said. "Providin' only that you cease callin' me 'Mester O'Neeell.' I'm not so much younger than you. I have heard never any but good of you. I hold you in my arms, and I'm going to kiss you, Mrs. Roosevelt. For now, and for the last time. It does not imply anything further. It's only because I want you to think of me as a friend, and a man you can trust; and I promise you I will never offer to kiss you again—assumin', that is, you do not come to my room and my bed some night. Is it agreed?"

A woman of fifty-seven was not ready to refuse what he offered. She had never been kissed, more than cousinly, by any man but Franklin. On the terms he stated, she did not refuse Kevin O'Neil. She raised her face toward him and let the big Irishman kiss her more than affectionately.

She lowered her head to his shoulder. "I trust you, Kevin," she said. "May God forgive me if I'm wrong."

Kevin drew the curtains across the windows of the bedroom. Then he switched on the electric light.

Mrs. Roosevelt showed him what she had looked at in the light of her flashlight.

"Paybook," he said. "An interestin' record. A sort of biography. My God, the man had an interestin' career."

Mrs. Roosevelt could not throw aside instantly the emotions he had generated in her, and she had to steel herself and focus on what he was saying. She was determined that what he had said would be true: that they had established trust in each other and there would be nothing more. It was not easy.

"Translatin' this," said Kevin, "it would appear our late friend served his Führer many ways, many places. He was, from 1925, a member of the *Nationalsozialistische Deutsche Arbeiterspartei.* An early member. Within two months after he joined the Party he joined the SS, with the rank of *Untersturmführer,* a sort of second lieutenant. That means he had money, probably also a university degree. He was a Berliner and was assigned to the Berlin headquarters of the SS. He was promoted twice before the Nazis came to power in 1933, then again in 1937 and 1940, which made him an *SS-Obersturmbannführer,* which is roughly equivalent to an army lieutenant colonel, as he told us. When he introduced himself to me, he called himself colonel."

"The other title has a certain stench to it," said Mrs. Roosevelt. "I myself am reluctant to use it, even to think it."

"I expect he understood that," said Kevin. "Let's see here, now. "In 1933 he joined the *Leibstandarte Adolf Hitler.* That's significant."

"What is it?" she asked.

"Hitler's personal bodyguard at first."

"Oh. That's why he said Hitler trusted him."

"Yes. He's a more important fellow than I realized. Going on with this . . . he suffered a heart attack in 1935 and was transferred to the *Reichs-Sicherheitshauptamt,* that is national police headquarters. In other words he was taken off rigorous military-type duty and assigned to administrative duties. In 1936 he was assigned to the *Sicherheitsdienst,* which is a special elite force within the SS, responsible for the internal security of the SS and the Nazi Party. Besides that, it is supposed to have foreign intelligence functions."

"That was an army uniform he was wearing, wasn't it?"

"The *Leibstandarte* became a regiment. It is a military unit, and its members wear the field gray, not black. Let's see here. Technically, *Obersturmbannführer* Brandt was still a member of the regiment. I am sure he took some pride in it."

"So that's what he was," said Mrs. Roosevelt. "But what did he *do?*"

"Well . . . In 1938 he was sent to Vienna, at first as an adjutant to Heydrich, who was there organizing the apparatus of repression; then, after Heydrich went on to other work, Brandt stayed and supervised the establishment of a permanent SD office for Austria. He did the same thing in Czechoslovakia and in Poland. Finally he was assigned to Vichy. The SD headquarters in Paris would be too big an office to be commanded by an *Obersturmbannführer*, so here he was. I would guess this assignment was something of a reward for him and semi-retirement as well. There are two references here to sick leave. He was fifty-two years old."

"Does it say if he was married or had children?"

"No. So— What else do we have?"

"He was carrying an unusually large amount of luggage for a man who was to be here only a day or two."

"Yes, and there was more in the car," said Kevin. "I doubt he planned to go back to Vichy. He was on his way to Berlin to do whatever it was he was going to do for us."

"Which might have been betray us," said Mrs. Roosevelt.

"Not likely, I think. Why would he come here and take part in an elaborate ruse?"

"Three suitcases," said Mrs. Roosevelt. "Everything in the wardrobe and bureau could be packed in one. Or two at the most."

Kevin picked up the suitcases and put them on the bed. They were not locked. He opened each. One of them was crammed with file folders filled with documents. Another contained what appeared to be scrapbooks, two of them. The third was empty.

"Interesting," said Mrs. Roosevelt as she opened the first scrapbook.

It was filled with pictures of Brandt. Apparently he had been a university professor in the 1920s. In the pictures he was wearing civilian clothes and in some of them smoking a pipe. His Nazi Party membership badge showed prominently in some of the pictures—a black swastika on white enamel, circled by a red band, then a gold one. In one picture he was wearing Alpine clothes: leather shorts held up by straps, a loose shirt, a conical hat with a big plume, wool socks to his knees, big hiking shoes. In that photograph and that one alone, a woman appeared. She stood beside him, but whether or not she was with him was not clear.

"Look at this," said Mrs. Roosevelt.

She showed Kevin a photograph of Brandt standing in an open car and giving the Nazi salute to Hitler, who was passing by in his big black Mercedes.

"Vienna," said Kevin. "The SS, SD, and Gestapo had been in town for three days before the Führer arrived. They had . . . pacified the city very efficiently before Hitler was exposed to the populace."

Another photograph, this one no snapshot but a picture obviously taken by a professional, showed Brandt shaking hands with *Reichsführer* Heinrich Himmler, watched by a dubious Heydrich.

Toward the end of the scrapbook Mrs. Roosevelt found pictures of Colonel Brandt in Paris. In one of those he was shaking hands with Hitler himself—the colonel bent forward in a slight bow, Hitler smiling so broadly that his teeth showed beneath his mustache. The photograph had been taken on that infamous day when the German Führer had spent a few triumphal hours in Paris, just after dawn, quickly viewing the Eiffel Tower, the Opera, and the Tomb of Napoleon, before rushing back to the airport and a return flight to Germany.

"Kevin— Look at this one."

She pointed to a picture of Brandt on the terrace here at Montrond, dressed in civilian clothes, chatting, apparently amiably, with Vivienne Duval.

"It may explain nothing more than why this château was chosen for our conference," said Kevin. "Or maybe that's what they were talking about in this picture: the arrangements for the conference."

"It is difficult to read anything into their expressions," said Mrs. Roosevelt. "Obviously, though, they have known each other for some time—at least long enough for this picture to be developed and printed and delivered to him for entry in his scrapbook."

He had been flipping through the second scrapbook.

"Th' photos there are interestin'," said Kevin. "Not nearly so interestin', though, as the ones in *this* scrapbook—which ye may not want to look at, Eleanor . . . They're not pretty."

"I am not squeamish," she said.

"How about prudish?"

"I am not that, either."

"Very well. I warned you."

He opened the second scrapbook. To the first several pages were affixed a dozen or so small snapshots. All of them were of women, and all of the women were naked.

One picture was of a long line of women standing as if for inspection—and in fact being inspected by some black-uniformed men, one of whom led a vicious-looking German shepherd dog on a tight leash. The photograph was too small to offer opportunity to judge any of the naked women; but it was apparent that they were of all ages; one or two, so far as the little picture showed, might have been as young as fourteen, while others looked as old as sixty.

What was going on was obvious enough. They were new inductees into a prison camp, standing on bleak open ground, probably on a cold day, being viewed—ogled would be a better word—by some of the officers of the camp.

Other pictures were of the more handsome ones, photographed individually or in groups of two or three. In these photos the faces could be seen: frightened and bewildered women, unable to believe that what was happening to them was real.

In three other pictures naked women were running, obviously as fast as they could.

"They're not tryin' to escape," said Kevin grimly. "They've been told that those who can run a certain distance in a certain time will be regarded as strong enough to work and will be given the privileges of workers: better food, better clothin', and so on."

"What of those who don't run fast enough?" asked Mrs. Roosevelt.

"We can't be sure. Likely they are put on subsistence rations.

Likely many of them die. We're bein' told—but it seems unbeliev-
able—that they are killed. The world couldn't contain anythin' that
bad, though. Could it?"

Mrs. Roosevelt shook her head. "No. It couldn't. Could it,
Kevin?"

"I am paid to try to find out," he said. "The Germans are very
firm on the subject. No such thing happens, they say. I hope it will
be possible to get these pictures out of France when we leave. And,
uh . . . There are more. Seen enough?"

"These pictures strengthen me in my determination," she
said.

"*Obersturmbannführer* Brandt was not a nice man," said
Kevin. "One has to wonder exactly why he collected these pictures."

Other photographs were of young women, conspicuously
frightened and unwilling to do what they were doing, posing awk-
wardly for someone's camera, displaying themselves on command.

Then there were others: the ones that caught Mrs. Roosevelt's interest more than any others.

This was a group of photographs showing a group of girls,
maybe a dozen of them, on their hands and knees, scrubbing a
sidewalk with brushes. All of them were stripped to panties and
brassieres. Their faces were contorted with the pain of humiliation. They were surrounded by a crowd of laughing people. In two
of the pictures a girl ran to or from a doorway, carrying a bucket.

It was exactly the scene Vicky had described: her own ago-
nizing humiliation on a Vienna street.

Mrs. Roosevelt wondered how many of these photographs
Colonel Brandt had taken himself, if he hadn't been in that guffaw-
ing crowd—if in fact he had not ordered the debasement of the
Jewish girls.

"Kevin . . ."

"Uhmm?"

Mrs. Roosevelt put her finger on one of the pictures. "Did
Vicky tell you she suffered exactly this, in Vienna in 1938?"

He shook his head. "No. She's said nothing of anything like that."

"Well, she told me. Because she is a Jew, she was compelled to do just what these girls are doing. I wonder if she is one of the girls in one of these pictures."

Kevin squinted over one of the photographs. "I don't see her. Three years? No, she couldn't be so different. But . . . This sort of thing didn't happen just one place. They made old men do the like. And women. Of course, it was the girls that they liked to make take off their clothes. Part of the game. They loved it. The Viennese loved it. Jews . . ."

"Do you have any idea to what extent Colonel Brandt was the initiator of this kind of thing?"

Kevin shook his head. "Not the business of the *Sicherheits-dienst*. I'd imagine Brandt wasn't there when this happened. I imagine he bought the pictures—or got them some such way. Or maybe he was a witness, with his camera. Maybe he made a point of going places where girls and women could be photographed undressed."

"Maybe she saw him," Mrs. Roosevelt suggested. "Maybe he . . . personally abused Vicky."

"And maybe she killed him, y're thinkin'?"

"Is that impossible?"

"It's possible, I suppose. So we have a suspect. Not a very good one, I think. But, on the other hand, the only one we have."

VI

KEVIN HAD PROMISED HE would never kiss Mrs. Roosevelt again, but he gave her a quick, cousinly peck on the cheek as he left her at the door to her room. He made not the slightest suggestion, by word or tone or gesture, that he would like to come in with her—so sparing her the necessity of a sharp negative.

They had agreed they would carry some of *Obersturmbann-führer* Brandt's papers and pictures to their rooms, for more thorough examination. With curtains drawn to hide the light, she sat on her bed and gave some of the materials a closer examination.

Kevin was right that none of the girls crawling in their underwear on the Vienna sidewalk was Vicky. Even so, Vicky could have been there, since it was obvious there was more activity than these particular photos showed. It was possible that she had been there, that Brandt had taken these pictures himself, and that there had been some kind of contact between them.

Vicky had said "worse things" had happened later, and Mrs. Roosevelt wondered if Brandt had had anything to do with those things.

She scanned some of the documents. Her German was far less than fluent. She had studied it at Allenswood, but it had been French the girls spoke at table, and the German all of them learned had been no more than what was considered appropriate for a girl

about to come out in society to know. That was to say, she should
be able to make a little affable conversation in German, to read and
to reply to a simple letter; but it was French, not German and not
English, that was the language of cultured mankind, as Mademoiselle Sylvestre had insisted, so the German had been given what
one of the American girls, from the West, had called "a lick and a
promise"—which impeded Mrs. Roosevelt's ability to read it now.

She could scan, even so. If she found anything interesting,
she could ask Kevin or Vicky to read it for her.

And, suddenly, there was something. A letter. It was addressed to *Obersturmbannführer* Artur Brandt, *Hauptamt der
SD*, Vichy. It was a letter in response to an inquiry, and it reported
that Duval, *Hauptmann* Emile, *Kriegsgefangener*—Captain Emile
Duval, prisoner of war—had died of his wounds, in a military hospital at Neuenkirchen on July 1, 1940.

So. Vivienne Lenclos Duval's husband had been dead almost
a year. Brandt had known it. Had he told her? Why had he in-
quired?

As she sat pondering, Mrs. Roosevelt heard the sound of
voices in the hall. Three A.M. Not likely to be insignificant.

She waited for the voices to fade. Then she took special care
in being quiet at opening her door.

Three people. Madame Vivienne Duval and two men. They
were at Colonel Brandt's door—*Obersturmbannführer* Brandt's
door. They opened and went in.

Three more people knew he was dead. Or knew, anyway, that
he was missing.

She could not sleep while Vicky was out somewhere—maybe by
now picked up by the police—so Mrs. Roosevelt sat in a chair in
her bedroom, tried to read more of the German documents, but
dozed fitfully and uncomfortably, her intervals of sleep marred by
the kind of nightmares that come when a person is half asleep and
half awake, knows the nightmare is not real, yet can't get rid of it.

Several times she dreamed she saw Vicky running across the

fields toward the château, pursued by men and dogs. This was a nightmare place where they had come, and nightmares were natural here.

When she saw light behind the closed curtains, she got up and swept the curtains back. She had a view of the river and fields from her windows, and as she stood, looking at a misty dawn, she saw Vicky for real, coming across a field of some new green crop, with Jeanine, both of them barefoot, with mud halfway to their knees.

"Madame Duval knows I've been out all night," said Vicky.

She had come to Mrs. Roosevelt's room, where Mrs. Roosevelt had ordered breakfast delivered as early as there was someone in the kitchen to respond to her urgent puffing into the whistle in the speaking tube. The food was of course for Vicky, and the young woman sat and ate hungrily.

"The countryside is alive with chickens," said Vicky ruefully. "Didn't you hear them crowing and cackling when the sun came up? Full of chickens. But the local people are hard put to get two eggs a week. You know what the French say? *Ils nous prennent tout.*' 'They're swiping everything.' A little thing like eggs. *Eggs*, for God's sake! Onto the trains for Germany. Don't German chickens lay eggs? What did the Krauts eat for eggs before they could steal them from the French?"

Mrs. Roosevelt had dressed in one of her khaki outfits. Somehow it seemed appropriate for the morning meeting she would soon have. While Vicky ate and talked, the First Lady stared at the countryside and found it difficult to believe that so handsome a land could lie under so oppressive a hand.

"I must ask you a question, Vicky."

"Any question you wish."

"*SS-Obersturmbannführer* Brandt . . . Did you know him before you came here?"

"I never knew him at all, alive. I never laid eyes on the man before I saw him lying dead on the floor."

"Is it possible you saw him and didn't know his name?"

"I couldn't know his face," said Vicky. "The bullet went in through the back of his head and burst his left eye. I promise you I did not look at the face any more than I had to."

"I'll show you a picture of him," said Mrs. Roosevelt. She opened one of the albums and chose the picture of Brandt in his Alpine costume. "There. Have you ever seen that man before?"

Vicky frowned over the photograph. "Never," she said.

"Well, then . . ."

Mrs. Roosevelt showed Vicky one of the photographs of girls in their underwear, scrubbing a sidewalk.

Vicky blanched. *"Where did you get this?"* she asked.

"He had it. Look at the rest of them. I don't see you there, but it is what you described to me."

Vicky blinked, and her eyes filled with tears. She put her finger on the image of a girl on her hands and knees. "Frederika," she whispered. "They killed her. Her father was a minister of the Austrian government, and they sent all of them to Sachsenhausen, where they all died."

"I'm sorry, Vicky," said Mrs. Roosevelt. "So you were there, but you weren't caught by the camera. Is that it?"

Vicky looked through the other pictures. "This was another day. But it is the same thing."

"They did this to you more than once?"

"More than once? Every day for a week. Only what they called the 'Jew-girls.' Not the Catholic bitches, except Frederika because her father had opposed the Nazis. They—"

"Maybe the other girls couldn't help it," Mrs. Roosevelt interrupted. *"They didn't—"*

"They stood around and laughed! Look at the pictures! Here! That is Maria! The blonde. She *laughed*! And she wasn't the only one."

Mrs. Roosevelt nodded. "These albums were in Colonel Brandt's room, in his luggage," she said. "I'd like to know if he took them or if he obtained them from someone else."

"I think I understand you," said Vicky bitterly. "You wonder if I didn't recognize my tormentor and take the first opportunity to kill him. Well . . . He was a swine. Isn't that obvious? But I didn't kill him. What's more, I wouldn't have, even if I had recognized him. Frederika is dead. But others are alive. I wouldn't throw away their lives for personal revenge. And I might add that I could have hoped you thought better of me than to suspect I would."

Mrs. Roosevelt sighed. "I owe you an apology, Vicky. I tender it."

Vicky ate hungrily of the eggs and potatoes that had been brought up supposedly as Mrs. Roosevelt's breakfast. "This is an unreal world," she said. "One where apologies—any fact any kind of civility—have lost all meaning. I drove that car last night to a farm about two kilometers from here. People hid the car under the hay in a barn. They couldn't offer a meal to two hungry women, because they didn't have food to offer. We drank coffee and ate a few scraps of bread. They know Jeanine is a Jew. They guessed I am. Even among them, some are anti-Semitic. They hid the car because they hated Brandt. If we had asked them to hide us, just us, I'm not sure they would have done it."

Mrs. Roosevelt listened intently. Her mind was filled with other things, but this deserved to be heard.

Vicky stopped. "Who killed him?" she asked.

"I wish we knew."

Vicky closed her eyes. "Maybe I did it. I can understand why you would wonder."

Mrs. Roosevelt shook her head. "Find out whatever you can about how many times Colonel Brandt came here before yesterday. If I am making a list of suspects, I must put Madame Duval on the list. I'll tell you why later. Find out what you can about the relationship between the colonel and our hostess."

"Wer kommt?" asked General Rommel.

They were meeting on the terrace—General Rommel, General Rousseau, without Gabrielle this time, Mrs. Roosevelt, Kevin

O'Neil, and Vivienne Duval—when the German general was first to notice a car coming along the river road.

The car turned off and approached the bridge that spanned the moat. Because that little bridge was reputedly weak, only an occasional motor vehicle crossed it. The car stopped just short, and the driver got out.

"Randolph Churchill?" asked Rommel.

"We may hope so," said General Rousseau.

The two generals had expressed their impatience with the nonappearance of the son of the Prime Minister.

"He is not extraordinarily bright, I am told," said Rommel, "and we can doubtlessly negotiate perfectly well without him; but it is irritating that the British see fit to withhold from us the token of their sincerity."

Though the German general used his own language, Mrs. Roosevelt understood what he meant. If she missed a word or two, his tone conveyed his meaning and his annoyance.

The driver hurried around the car and opened the door on the passenger side. A tall, attractive, auburn-haired young woman climbed out. She walked across the bridge and into the château.

She appeared on the terrace a minute later. *"Bonjour,"* she said, nodding first to Mrs. Roosevelt, then to the two generals, finally to Kevin and to Vivienne Duval. *"Je regrette de vous faire attendre. Je suis* Sarah Churchill."

No one was able to conceal surprise.

Sarah Churchill went on, still speaking French—"My brother became ill suddenly on Tuesday and is unable to come here. My father then asked me to come. In all frankness, I am more intelligent and better informed than my brother, so you need not be dismayed at my coming in his stead."

General Rousseau stiffened in indignation at the impertinence of this brazen young woman. He settled an irate stare on her.

This had to be translated for General Rommel, which Kevin did. The German general stared at the young woman, tipped his head a bit, and showed his faint, tight smile. He let her see his amused condescension. *"Es freut mich,"* he said. It was a pleasure to meet her.

"Meinerseits, Herr General," she said. The pleasure is mine.

She turned to Mrs. Roosevelt and extended both her hands to clasp Mrs. Roosevelt's extended hand. "It's a great pleasure to meet you," she said. "I've spent a lot of time in America, and I know how much affection people have for you."

Madame Duval offered Sarah Churchill some breakfast, and Sarah said she would enjoy a piece of fruit of any kind, if it was available, with perhaps a cup of coffee.

The group sat down in chairs on the terrace. It was a pleasant place for a meeting.

"But where is Colonel Brandt?" asked General Rousseau.

Vivienne Duval answered, shaking her head. "He has left, *Monsieur le Général,*" she said. "He left sometime before dawn."

General Rousseau stood up. "We have been betrayed," he said. "The police will descend on us—"

Mrs. Roosevelt had prepared herself for this moment. "I think not," she said. "If police were coming, they would have been here a long time ago."

General Rommel seemed to be catching the gist of the conversation, but Kevin translated rapidly for him.

"I think I had best return immediately to Paris," said General Rousseau.

"Monsieur le Général," said Mrs. Roosevelt firmly. "If we have been betrayed, returning to Paris will do you no good whatever. If Colonel Brandt has given an account of our meeting to the Gestapo, you will be arrested there just as readily as here."

General Rousseau hesitated, frowning darkly.

"Sie hat Recht," said Rommel. *"Ich bleibe."* She is right. I am staying.

General Rousseau glowered. Then he shrugged. "Yes. As far as it goes, she is correct. But I think we are doomed."

"In the meanwhile," said Sarah Churchill, "would it not be wise to carry along the discussions we came here for? All of you have assumed great risks in coming here. I myself had the horrifying experience of parachuting from an airplane in the dark. I would be most unhappy if it turned out to be for nothing."

"What can we do," asked General Rousseau, "if the representative of the German security apparatus has withdrawn from the discussions? Who is going to rid us of the tyrant?"

Rommel's expression suggested he probably understood what the French general had just said, but he waited for Kevin's translation and then said—"That has to be a German problem, and you need not concern yourself with it. *We* are the ones who must take the greatest risk. The worst that can happen to you is that the status quo continues. There are a number of ways of setting the Führer aside. Able and courageous men are working on it."

"Setting him aside . . ." said Kevin after he had translated. "Does that mean he is not to be assassinated?"

"What difference does it make," asked Rommel, "if he is dead or in prison or is honorably retired, so long as German forces withdraw from France and so on?"

"What assurance can we have that you will not come again?" asked General Rousseau.

"If you are suggesting you mean to demand our disarmament, as you did in 1918 and enforced against us in 1919, then this meeting is over and we can all go back to our duties. Germany will never accept that humiliation again. If you mean to reduce us to helplessness, then defeat us!"

"We were more generous to you at Versailles in 1919 than you were to us at Compiègne in 1940," said General Rousseau.

"If you had been more generous to us in 1919, there need not have been a Compiègne," said Rommel.

"We will achieve nothing by exchanging bitter observations on old injustices," said Mrs. Roosevelt. "Whom are you proposing as the new head of the German state, *Herr General*?"

"Someone who will do what must be done, yet will be acceptable to the German people," said Rommel.

"Who?"

"It could be any one of a number of men. At the moment I should think the leading candidate would be *Herr Reichsmarschall* Göring."

"I am not certain that would be acceptable to the French nation," said General Rousseau after he heard the translation.

"What is acceptable to France is a matter of total indifference to us," said Rommel coldly. "I represent officers who control the army and can control the state. We are willing to sign an agreement for withdrawal of our forces from France and other countries—which, allow me to suggest, *Monsieur le Général*, should be your chief concern. How we govern ourselves is no concern of yours at all."

"How serious do you regard it," asked Sarah Churchill, "that the representative of the SS and SD has withdrawn from this conference?"

"If he has not in fact gone somewhere to summon in SS troops to arrest us all, it is not very significant," said Rommel. *"Obersturmbannführer* Brandt could have been helpful to us at critical moments. In the end, though, the *Wehrmacht* will have to fight the SS. Blood will be shed, but the *Wehrmacht* will overwhelm the Führer's little private army."

"Are you suggesting," Kevin asked, "that Germany is to remain the greatest military power in Europe?"

"You fear my country," said Rommel. "But I believe, *Fräulein* Churchill, it is your own honored father who has warned repeatedly about the chief threat to Europe. The Bolsheviks. Stalin is the menace. Germany stands as your guard against him."

"That will be easier to accept," said Sarah Churchill, "when your Führer is gone."

"That is what we are here to discuss," said Rommel.

"I must return to the subject of the Jews," said Mrs. Roosevelt in French.

"Jews, Jews!" complained General Rousseau. "Damn the Jews! I am here to talk about France!"

Rommel didn't wait for Kevin's translation. "Let us not let the question of Jews become an obstacle in the way of ending the war before we are all destroyed by the Bolsheviks."

A black car drove along the road and entered the grounds of the château. The driver fairly leaped from it and strode stiffly across the bridge. He wore the black uniform of the SS, complete with red swastika armband.

Rommel watched him approach. "There is no point in fleeing," he said. "No point in killing him."

A minute or so later the man strode onto the terrace and raised his arm in a salute to General Rommel. *"Herr General! Ich bin Hauptsturmführer* Konrad Giesel. *Ist Herr Obersturmbannführer* Brandt *nicht hier?"*

Rommel told him that Brandt had left during the night.

Giesel glanced around. He smiled wanly. "Be calm," he said. "I know who you are and why you are here. I am *Obersturmbannführer* Brandt's adjutant. He trusts me. So can you."

Mrs. Roosevelt judged this man less trustworthy than Brandt—though why she should think so was unclear in her mind. He was younger than Brandt, not much more than thirty, she guessed. No hair showed beneath his black SS cap, but his eyebrows and lashes were pale blond. His face and body were what Americans called "chunky"—which was to say that he was husky, solid, and broad. His face was in fact square. His lips were thick. He was, at this moment, intensely self-conscious.

"Obersturmbannführer Brandt left during the night," said Rommel in German. "He left no explanation as to why. He left no warning, either. We assume he had good reason."

Giesel clicked his heels together and nodded curtly. "Thank you, *Herr General.* In his absence, I will stay and hear what is said, so that I can report the conversation to him."

Rommel nodded, equally curtly.

Giesel wore a holster on his belt, the leather covering a small pistol. "Are discussions going well?" he asked in French.

"Quite well, I think we can say," said Sarah Churchill.

"I don't believe I know who you are, *Fräulein,*" said Giesel.

"I am Sarah Churchill. My brother was taken ill and could not come," she said in German. "My father asked me to come."

Giesel bowed more deeply to her than he had to the others. "Ah, so. And I recognize Mrs. Roosevelt and General Rousseau." He spoke to Kevin. "You would be Kevin O'Neil. And, of course, the delightful Madame Duval I do know."

Their chairs were situated in a sort of circle. There was one for Giesel, and he sat down.

"Colonel Brandt did not mention your name," said Mrs. Roosevelt to the young SS officer.

Giesel put his cap aside, revealing the bristle cut of his pale hair. "I should hope not," he said. He spoke heavily accented French. "It was necessary for him to mention yours to me, not mine to you. I think I don't need to remind you of the risk we are taking here."

"Yes. I suppose you are taking a greater risk than I," said Mrs. Roosevelt.

Giesel frowned and glanced around the group. "I cannot imagine," he said, "why *Obersturmbannführer* Brandt is not here. I cannot imagine where he has gone."

"Neither can we," said Vivienne Duval.

"Left in the night, you say?"

"Not long before dawn, *Herr Hauptsturmführer,*" said Vivienne Duval. "I was asleep and was wakened by a flash of light on the curtains of my bedroom. I rose and went to the window to see what the light was. It was the headlamps of a car. The car was being turned around, and shortly it was driven away. Not until this morning did I realize it was *Herr Obersturmbannführer* Brandt's car."

"But he made no suggestion to anyone last night that he would be going away during the night?" asked Giesel.

Some of the group shook their heads.

"The household staff," said Giesel. "Have you questioned them? Did anyone arrive with a message for the *Obersturmbann-führer?*"

"I have not yet asked," said Vivienne Duval.

"I should like to question your staff, then. That the *Obersturmbannführer* should have left so abruptly, without a word to anyone, is quite mysterious. In fact, our safety may be involved. Is it possible he was arrested in the night?"

"Officers arriving to arrest him would have had to get into the château by ringing the bell," said Vivienne Duval. "The gate on this side of the bridge is kept locked at night."

Giesel nodded, but he remained skeptically thoughtful. "On the other hand," he said, "I do not suppose you claim the château is impenetrable except through that gate. Agents arriving to arrest him might have wanted to enter quietly, so as not to alarm him before they reached him. They could have climbed over the wall, could they not?"

"Yes, with a ladder," said Vivienne Duval.

"You may be assured," said Giesel dryly, "that if Gestapo agents came with such a purpose in mind, they would have had the foresight to bring a ladder."

"Have you reason to think Colonel Brandt has been arrested?" asked Mrs. Roosevelt.

"No. But there were questions yesterday as to where he was."

"Will you advise your office that he is missing?"

Giesel shook his head. "I don't think that would be a very good idea. No. He may return at any time. Meanwhile, I will question the household staff."

A light rain began to fall, so lunch was served in a small, bright dining room with broad windows that overlooked the Loire. It was the room where a painted portrait of a saucy bare-breasted woman hung above a small, marble-faced fireplace.

Noticing that her guests were beguiled by the painting, Vivienne Duval said, "It is of a woman known to us only as Françoise. She lived here in the last two decades of the seventeenth century, as mistress of the then Count of Persigny."

The gilt-framed painting was of a horizontal oval shape. The handsome woman was dressed in an elaborate green gown, loose and modest except that it had been pulled down in front to expose her breasts. Her hair was tightly curled. A little spaniel lay on her lap. She smiled as she tossed flowers to two naked winged cherubs in the air to either side of her.

"It has always been attributed to Mignard," said Vivienne Duval. "More likely, it is a Gascar. According to such records as have survived, as much as one-third of the furniture now in the château was purchased by Françoise, and most of the chief rooms were redecorated to her taste. In the 1850s, the then owners of the château had her painted over, so she would not appear so immodest. The repainting was so crude that the picture was banished into storage. My grandfather had it removed from storage in 1925, cleaned and restored, and rehung where we believe it had hung for more than one hundred fifty years."

"Charmante," said Gabrielle, who had joined General Rousseau for lunch.

"She was a contemporary of Sarah, first Duchess of Marlborough," said Vivienne Duval. "There is a painting of Sarah in the National Portrait Gallery in London, so similar in style that it is believed the two were painted by the same artist, within a few months of each other."

Mrs. Roosevelt had taken a bite or two of her chicken when a servant approached Madame Duval and spoke quietly.

Vivienne Duval rose and came to Mrs. Roosevelt, to whisper in her ear, "Your maid asks to see you immediately. It seems two guests have arrived and expect to see you."

Mrs. Roosevelt left the dining room and went to meet the people described as her guests in the library of the château.

She found them there. Vicky was with them. One of the women was immediately recognizable. She was Gertrude Stein.

Mrs. Roosevelt surmised that the other one was Alice B. Toklas.

She would have known Gertrude Stein by appearance even if she had never met her, which she had since the famous writer had made a tour of the States in 1934, shortly after publication of *The Autobiography of Alice B. Toklas*, her most famous work. Gertrude Stein was sixty-seven years old, a big, broad-framed, heavyset woman, who wore her hair almost as close-cropped as a Prussian sergeant. She was a bona fide eccentric, who had compelled the world to accept her on her own terms. Her reputation rested more on the salon she had made of her Paris apartment and on the art she had collected since she came to Paris more than thirty years ago than on her literary achievement. She had bought Picasso and Matisse when no one bought Picasso or Matisse, and the Picasso portrait of her was world famous.

She was of course an American Jew, from San Francisco. Staying in France after the German victory in 1940 had put her in jeopardy of freedom and life. Even so, she had not abandoned the country where she had lived since shortly after the turn of the century; and, with her devoted friend, Alice B. Toklas, she remained, living quietly in a country house at Bilignin, a few kilometers from the Swiss frontier.

"Miss Stein says you have met," said Vicky. "But you have not met Miss Alice Toklas."

Mrs. Roosevelt smiled, greeted both women, and shook their hands. She stood half a foot taller than either of them. Alice B. Toklas was a slender, diminutive woman with a chronic gloomy air. She murmured a word of greeting and left it to Gertrude Stein to speak.

"I am very pleased to see you," said Mrs. Roosevelt. "I must ask how you come to be here. An officer of one of the most dreaded of the German security services told me you were coming."

"There is," said Gertrude Stein somewhat loftily, "a community of people devoted to what is worthwhile in life. Germans are to be found in that community. Why not? No people is to be judged by its politics."

"I will accept that," said Mrs. Roosevelt. "I have to emphasize, however, that my presence in France is a national secret; and I have to ask how and why you came to know I am here."

"The information came to me through people we mutually trust," said Gertrude Stein. "Through people who merit our trust. You need not worry that our meeting will compromise your mission here."

"You know what that is?" asked Mrs. Roosevelt.

"You are here on a mission to attempt to restore peace," said Gertrude Stein. "There is only one value greater than peace."

"And that is?"

"Humanity."

"Unless I mistake you, Miss Stein, you are talking about an effort to save the Jews of France."

"Or any other Jews. Do you know why Alice and I are free? Only because it would create a terrible scandal if we were arrested. The Nazis will make small concessions to keep the United States out of the war. That is our safety. We are a small concession. If the United States becomes a belligerent—as I believe it must and will—then Alice Toklas and I will be arrested and shipped to a concentration camp."

"Do you want to accompany me when I leave France?" asked Mrs. Roosevelt.

Gertrude Stein shook her head firmly. "I left the States almost forty years ago, for very good reason. The French have been good to me. I could have left last year. Alice and I talked it over and decided to retreat only as far as our country place. And there we remain—and hear stories of horrors being perpetrated by . . . Perpetrated by the Vichy government as much, almost, as by the Germans themselves."

Mrs. Roosevelt glanced toward the door of the library. "Important men are suspending important discussions while we talk, Miss Stein. What can I do for you?"

"I want to send vital information to the States," said Gertrude Stein. "It is utterly inconceivable to me that Americans should not know, and maybe not care, what is happening to European Jews. I believe they *will* care . . . when they receive the information from someone whose voice they are willing to hear. Maybe that voice is mine."

"In our talks, a principal topic is the fate of the Jews," said Mrs. Roosevelt.

"If your talks fail and the war goes on, what then? Will the cowardice of American pacifists overwhelm the will of the American people to stand for justice? For humanity?"

"I will carry your message," said Mrs. Roosevelt.

"You don't *have* my message," said Gertrude Stein. "I need time to talk to you."

"That may depend on the attitude of the woman who lives in this château," said Mrs. Roosevelt.

Gertrude Stein shook her head. "We will have the complete and enthusiastic cooperation of Vivienne Lenclos Duval. She is a woman of exemplary courage. Her father, Julien Lenclos, fled France in 1940 because his mother, Vivienne's grandmother, was a Jew. This is enough to place Vivienne on a transport to Poland."

"What about the others?" asked Mrs. Roosevelt. "Do the others know you are here?"

"The man with the gross title, *Obersturmbannführer* Brandt, knows. He made it possible for us to travel here."

"Unfortunately, Brandt is not here. He left suddenly last night. Do you know a man called *Hauptsturmführer* Giesel?"

Gertrude Stein shook her head.

"Miss Stein," said Vicky. "I will take you to a suite where I am sure you and Miss Toklas will be comfortable. When Mrs. Roosevelt can find the time, she will hear what you have to say."

VII

"DAMN!" GROWLED KEVIN. "HOW many more people know we are here?"

"Miss Stein and Miss Toklas are risking their lives as much as we are risking ours," said Mrs. Roosevelt.

"Two old Jewish women," said Vicky. "Also, sexual deviants. They fall into, not just one but two, of the categories of people the Nazis hate the most. Besides which, those two women have given the Nazis good reason to hate them even more. They're a pair of heroines. So, if you want to know who let them know we are here and who arranged their coming, it was yours truly. *I* did it. I'm hoping they will choose to leave France when you do, go with you."

"Miss Stein says she will not leave France," said Mrs. Roosevelt.

"She has no great love for the United States of America," said Vicky. "Can you imagine how the America of ten, twenty, thirty years ago reacted to a woman like her: a big, heavy Jewish girl with an amorous inclination to other girls? Think of being what she is and living in the America of William Jennings Bryan and Billy Sunday, not to mention Aimee Semple McPherson. I'm not sure she finds the Nazis much more despicable than some of her fellow Americans."

"You say you arranged for these two women to come here," said Kevin. "Do you want to tell us why?"

"I would like to get them out of France, whether they say they want to go or not. It is only a matter of time, I'm afraid, before they will be killed."

"You say they're heroines," said Mrs. Roosevelt. "Do you mean they're doing humanitarian work?"

"Their country home is not too far from the Swiss border. They've got contacts. They've managed to get some people across, out of France."

"It seems," said Kevin, "that you've got your own agenda for this meetin'. Does Wild Bill Donovan know that?"

Vicky shrugged. "I am not employed by Colonel Donovan."

"Does General Rousseau know?"

"Yes."

"And Colonel Brandt knew," said Mrs. Roosevelt.

"Yes. He was the source of the passes they are carrying, allowing them to travel. Papers endorsed by an *Obersturmbannführer* of the *Sicherheitsdienst* carry a lot of weight with Vichy policemen."

"Are we to understand that you had worked with Colonel Brandt before?"

"No, not personally. He has extended cooperation to certain friends of mine."

"Of the *Résistance*," said Mrs. Roosevelt.

Vicky nodded.

"Then his death is a great misfortune," said the First Lady. "In fact— Will Miss Stein and Miss Toklas be able to return home without some further document they expected to obtain from him?"

"Their pass authorized them to travel to Vichy and return. It says Miss Toklas requires medical treatment at a Vichy hospital."

"I'll be glad to give some attention to the fact that Brandt is dead," said Kevin. "Somebody besides us knows it, and it's damned important we find out who."

"I'm uncomfortable about *Hauptsturmführer* Giesel questioning the household staff," said Vicky. "If he investigates carefully enough, and thoroughly enough, he might find out that Brandt is dead."

"In which case," said Kevin, "he'll no longer be on our side of things."

"Apart from Jeanine, is it likely that any of the other servants know of the death of Colonel Brandt?" asked Mrs. Roosevelt.

"No," said Vicky. "And if they do know, would they tell? I doubt they would. But we can't be sure."

"I feel reasonably confident no one saw us carrying the body out," said Kevin.

"Who heard the gunshot?" asked Mrs. Roosevelt.

"If you didn't, or Kevin didn't, it's unlikely anybody else did," said Vicky. "I live in the servant's quarters, and I can tell you for sure I didn't hear it there."

"I've wondered about this," said Mrs. Roosevelt. "I was in bed and may have dozed off. On the other hand, I heard your knock on the door distinctly enough. How could I have missed a pistol shot? These walls and doors aren't so thick that— Could it have been a silenced weapon?"

"There's no such thing," said Kevin. "A suppressor on a pistol can reduce the sound very substantially, but there's no such thing as a pistol that fires silently."

"The doors *are* heavy," said Mrs. Roosevelt. "The walls are thick. Could the, uh . . . suppressor so far reduce the sound that I wouldn't have heard it three rooms away?"

"Or reduce it so much that General Rousseau and Gabrielle in the next room wouldn't have heard it? Or that General Rommel across the hall wouldn't have heard it?" asked Vicky.

"Who sleeps where, exactly?" asked Kevin.

Mrs. Roosevelt made a small sketch—

Kevin nodded over the little drawing. "Okay. Nothing more than two oak doors separated Brandt from Rousseau or Rommel. That means a sound suppressor on the pistol. The weapon that sent a bullet in the back of Brandt's head and out through his face was no air pistol. I'd guess nine millimeter. *That'd* make an explosion. There had to be a suppressor. Which means a fairly sophisticated weapon. No on-the-spot angry shooting."

"No quick argument resulting in death," said Mrs. Roosevelt.

Kevin shook his head. "The kind of weapon the Gestapo would bring—which is an idea that scares the hell out of me."

"Why," asked Mrs. Roosevelt, "would the Gestapo come in the night, kill Colonel Brandt, leave his body, and go away, making no further inquiry?"

"We can't say they've made no further inquiry," said Kevin. "They just haven't made any—any that is apparent—since early this morning."

They were taking a short break before lunch, these three in Mrs. Roosevelt's bedroom. Gertrude Stein and Alice B. Toklas had been installed in another wing of the château, where their presence need not be noted by General Rommel.

The German general had expressed an interest in a half-hour's nap before lunch. The French general had smiled at that and had hurried off to his room, where Gabrielle waited for him. Sarah Churchill had expressed her gratitude for a break and a rest.

Mrs. Roosevelt had called her two associates to her room for a review.

"I've learned something else you should know," said Vicky. "The murder room has been locked. I got a key from Jeanine and had a look. Everything the *Obersturmbannführer* brought here— clothes, luggage, whatever you left last night—has been removed. There is no trace of him in the room, no sign he ever entered that room."

"Who removed—?"

"Two men who work here. The gardener and a general factotum. They carried everything to a room in one of the corner towers."

"By order of Madame Duval?" asked Mrs. Roosevelt.

"By order of Madame Duval."

Mrs. Roosevelt stared out over the courtyard and the wall of the château, toward the river and the French countryside beyond. "It is, I think, imperative," she said, "that we conclude our discussions as soon as possible and call for our return transportation. Something ugly is going to happen here."

"Uglier than murder?" asked Vicky.

"I've seen murder before," said Mrs. Roosevelt. "But always before, I hoped the police would find out who did it—and did what I could to help them find out. This is altogether different. The generals should be able to resolve their differences this afternoon."

Vicky shook her head. "Military differences are the least of it," she said.

"Ah, *Monsieur le Hauptsturmführer,*" the First Lady said to Giesel, haphazardly mixing French and German. Going on in French, she asked, "Were your inquiries of the household staff useful?"

Giesel shook his head. "They profess to know nothing."

"If you remain as a guest in the château this evening, that may become more comprehensible," she said. "No lights are left burning at night. The place is dark and silent. In my judgment, Colonel Brandt could have left, carrying his luggage, and driven away in his car, without anyone noticing—except, of course, Madame Duval, who saw the lights from his car."

"I need hardly explain," said Giesel stiffly, "why I cannot make the usual inquiries about the whereabouts of *Obersturmbannführer* Brandt. I cannot activate the apparatus of the *Reichs-Sicherheitshauptamt* to locate a missing officer of the SD."

"No, I suppose your situation is very awkward," said Mrs. Roosevelt.

"Sie haben Recht, gnädige Frau," said Giesel in German he obviously hoped she understood.

Appreciating that he felt more comfortable with anyone who spoke his language, she said, *"Ja, es ist peinlich."*

"I believe in my Führer," said Giesel, returning to the French he knew she understood. *"Il est un dieu."* He is a god. "His name will endure forever as the greatest man my country has ever produced. But . . . success generates hubris, does it not? He has conquered France. Yes, France and all the rest of the traditional enemies of the Fatherland. Is it not enough? The greatness of the Führer must be preserved by a few of us who are ready to restrain him and return him to reality. General Rommel is one of those few. So is *Obersturmbannführer* Brandt and a few others whose names I should not mention. We do not apologize for the recovery of our nation and people from the impositions placed on us at Versailles. We owe that to our Führer. We will restrain him and enshrine him."

The contradiction struck Mrs. Roosevelt forcibly. But she strained to appear understanding, nodded thoughtfully, and said, "Every great man needs someone to tell him when he is wrong. Think of Caesar. Think of Napoleon."

"Yes! Yes!" said Giesel excitedly. "You understand perfectly."

The question was, how long would it be before *he* really understood?

She reviewed the situation in her bathroom—where she had privacy—before going down for lunch.

Shot in the back of the head with a silenced—all right, sound-suppressed, pistol—in his bedroom in the château. About midnight. But only a minute or two after he had used the speaking tube to order a bottle of brandy.

Who?

Who had reason enough to want him dead? Too many people. She wrote a list and scanned it before she wadded it up and flushed it down the toilet. On the list—

—The Gestapo, which had learned what he was doing.

—Giesel, who might have come to the château in the night with orders to kill a traitor. But—

——Traitor to which cause?

——Traitor to the Third Reich?

——Traitor to associates in the German security apparatus?

——Traitor to the French and allied people who were risking their lives here?

—General Rommel, who did not trust him and whose career and life depended on Brandt's silence.

—General Rousseau, who had to see him as a deadly enemy, not just of France but of all France stood for.

—Viktoria Neustadt, who maybe recognized him as the man who had caused her humiliation on the streets of Vienna, followed by worse things that happened to her family.

—Kevin O'Neil. God knew who he was, really.

—Madame Vivienne Lenclos Duval, who knew Brandt from time before this conference.

—Giesel, as agent for any of half the people listed before.

The list went down with the flush water. It had been a useful discipline for the mind, but she dared not keep it and risk someone else's seeing it.

Before she was entirely ready to go back downstairs, Mrs. Roosevelt was alerted by a discreet rap on her door. She opened it to find Sarah Churchill. The young woman glanced up and down the hall and with a conspiratorial air entered the First Lady's room.

"I wanted a chance to talk with you alone," she said.

"Please have a chair."

"Thank you . . . Does it occur to you that you and I may be the only two sane people in this château?"

"I don't quite see it that way," said Mrs. Roosevelt.

Sarah sat down and settled her striking green eyes on the First Lady. She smiled. She was stylishly dressed in a white silk blouse and a pleated tartan skirt, in spite of the fact she had parachuted into France from a small airplane and sneaked to Montrond in the trunk of a car. She exuded self-confidence. Mrs. Roosevelt remembered of her the story that she was married to a Viennese music-hall comedian twice her age, reputed to be a Jew. Sarah had come to America to marry, pursued by her brother Randolph, who had hired American lawyers to try to prevent the marriage. Another element of her life story was that she had danced "as nearly naked as the law allows"—as the newspapers had put it at the time—as a member of the chorus in a London revue.

That her father had sent this young woman on this mission was ample evidence of how important Prime Minister Churchill thought it was. If something bad happened, she would at the very least be held as a hostage for the remainder of the war. That she was here was evidence of her courage, too.

"My father told me to beware," said Sarah. "He asked me to warn you, too."

"Of what, specifically?" asked Mrs. Roosevelt.

"Of the people Colonel Donovan assigned to you," said Sarah. "Particularly of Kevin O'Neil."

"What of Mr. O'Neil?"

"He's an Irish soldier of fortune," said Sarah. "He is here because he is being paid."

"Yes. Ten thousand pounds, I believe."

"Oh— You know that."

"He calls himself a mercenary."

"Well, then. How favorably are you impressed with Viktoria Neustadt?"

"Quite favorably," said Mrs. Roosevelt.

Sarah nodded and smiled. "She impresses me well, too. But I

think we have to keep in mind how she is motivated. By hatred. By implacable hatred."

"She has reason."

"Reason is the point," said Sarah. "I hope it hasn't made her irrational. Given my choice, I suppose I'd rather put my trust in a mercenary than a fanatic."

"I'm not sure we have to make that sort of choice," said Mrs. Roosevelt calmly.

"All right. Father asked me to remind you that General Rommel was for a time a member of Herr Hitler's personal staff. The two men apparently think rather well of each other."

"I was informed of that before I left Washington."

"Were you told to expect Gabrielle?"

"No. She is a surprise."

"To me, too," said Sarah. "General Paul Rousseau has always kept a mistress. She is apparently just the latest. But I would like to get word back to London that she is here and see if we can determine who she is."

"Is it important?"

Sarah shrugged. "One of his mistresses, of twenty-five years ago, was of some importance."

"Who was that?" Mrs. Roosevelt asked.

Sarah grinned. "Have you ever heard of Gertrud Margarete Zelle?" she asked.

"I don't believe so."

"She was better known by her stage name. Mata Hari. General Rousseau might have been ruined by the scandal of having his name associated with hers—except that the names of the minister of war and several other generals were linked to her name, too. I hope Gabrielle is not the Mata Hari of *this* war."

Mrs. Roosevelt sighed. "Yes. Well, I suppose we had better rejoin the generals."

"I'd think there is no hurry," said Sarah. "The generals have to negotiate the terms. I'm not sure exactly what your role here is, but I know mine. I am here only to assure General Rommel and

General Rousseau that my father's government is in good faith in supporting this effort. I hope maybe your role has a little more dignity than mine. I *know* why I am here. I am a hostage."

"Oh, really, my dear, I—"

"No. That's what I am. My brother was to have been General Rommel's assurance that commandos won't drop in on this château and kidnap him. Indeed, I was surprised to find he spent last night here, when my brother didn't appear. He seems to accept me as a substitute."

"I am here as an observer," said Mrs. Roosevelt. "In a sense, I suppose I am a hostage as well as you. My presence is a token of my husband's good faith, but I am also to observe and report in detail. I have also found an issue I wish to press."

"The fate of the Jews," said Sarah with a degree of skepticism.

"Yes. The peace settlement must have its humanitarian side. We cannot be satisfied with German withdrawal from France, the Low Countries, and so on unless—"

"Is that United States policy?"

"I am not sure there *is* a United States policy, except that the peace must be peace with justice. Without justice, there can be no peace, only another truce, then another war."

"With all due respect, Mrs. Roosevelt," said Sarah in a cool tone, "if you lived in London you might be willing to sacrifice some justice to get the bombing stopped."

"We can discuss it later," said the First Lady.

Rain continued to fall, so the afternoon meeting was held in the library of the château, overlooked by a periwigged Count of Persigny staring down from a gilt frame above the fireplace. The library was a two-story room, with a narrow gallery running all the way around to give access to the books shelved on the upper level. Mrs. Roosevelt resolved to spend some time in the room before she left Montrond, examining the books. There were thousands of volumes, most of them leather bound; and she could see that, while most of them were in French, many were in German, English, and Latin—indeed, she could see a few in Greek.

The discussions between the two generals went surprisingly smoothly, probably because they were two coldly logical professionals who, except for the patriotism expected of men of their calling, could discuss the movement of boundaries and the fate of peoples with virtually no emotion.

They agreed on what they considered the essentials of a peace, in much the same terms as they had used yesterday.

Germany would withdraw from France. That was of course what General Rousseau most wanted, and once that point was firmly settled, he was flexible. Both nations would return prisoners of war: a German concession, since France had no Germans as prisoners. The withdrawing German army would not carry away French property. Property already taken, such as industrial machinery, would be returned. Works of art would be returned. General Rommel said there might have to be a few small exceptions to that, since some of the works were in the hands of *Reichsmarschall* Göring, a man whose cooperation they would probably need. France would demand no reparations from Germany.

Mrs. Roosevelt did not intervene in the discussion. If what they were discussing could be achieved, the war would end; and that, after all, was the chief end of the conference. Certain facts impressed themselves forcibly on her mind, just the same. France and Britain had gone to war in 1939 to defend Poland. But no one was here to speak for Poland. What was more, General Rousseau obviously cared nothing for Poland. He wanted German withdrawal from Belgium, Luxembourg, and The Netherlands, because that was essential to French security; but he said nothing about the Germans liberating Denmark or Norway, much less Czechoslovakia or Poland.

No one spoke even for Italy, and she wondered how Signor Mussolini would react when and if he was informed of the agreement being made here.

Sarah Churchill, though she called herself a hostage and not even an observer, was not reticent. "When does submarine warfare stop?" she asked in German.

Rommel nodded at her and smiled. "When the Royal Navy no longer blockades German ports, all U-boats will return to those ports," he said.

"And when does the Blitz stop?" she asked.

"It already has, hadn't you noticed? The *Luftwaffe* has been shifted to the east. That's why it's so urgent that we reach an agreement here. An attack on Russia could begin in the next ten days."

"Miss Churchill . . . or Mrs. Oliver—"

"I prefer Miss Churchill," said Sarah.

"Mrs. Roosevelt would like to see you in her room."

Sarah Churchill nodded at Vicky, then glanced around to be sure no one was listening and asked, "What's happened with *Obersturmbannführer* Brandt?"

"He left," said Vicky. "Decamped in the night."

"Do you suppose he lost his nerve when my brother didn't show up?"

"I don't know."

"Who is this fellow *Hauptsturmführer* Giesel? Is he supposed to be taking Brandt's place?"

"Possibly."

"Brandt is essential to the plot," said Sarah, her voice so low it was almost a whisper. "He is the man who can get close to Hitler."

Vicky shook her head. "I don't know what's going on," she said. "Everybody thinks Brandt will return shortly."

"He had better. Why does Mrs. Roosevelt want me? Do you know?"

"She didn't say."

A couple of minutes later, Sarah knocked on Mrs. Roosevelt's bedroom door and was admitted by the First Lady, who opened the door only enough to let the two young women, Sarah and Vicky, slip through.

"*Gertrude Stein!*"

"Hello, Sarah."

"We've met, of course," said Sarah to Mrs. Roosevelt. "She's written a piece or two for the stage, you know. It's good to see you, Gertrude. And Alice. My God! What a risk you are taking being here!"

"We all are," said Gertrude Stein. She had not risen to greet Sarah, as Alice Toklas did, but took her hand and shook it warmly, then kissed it.

Gertrude Stein had a characteristic way of sitting in an upholstered chair. She sat with both feet flat on the floor, settling her bulk fully into the yielding chair; and, with an expression sometimes lugubrious, she looked like a hen sitting on eggs.

"Well," breathed Sarah. "How are you two? What have you been doing?"

"Surviving," said Alice B. Toklas simply.

"We try not to call attention to ourselves," said Gertrude Stein.

"Miss Stein has come here to give us some information," said Mrs. Roosevelt. "Actually, she came to give it to me, but I think you should hear it, Sarah. I think you should report it directly and in detail to your father."

Sarah nodded and sat down facing Gertrude Stein.

"We cannot," said the bigger, older woman, "close our eyes and ears to what is happening. We cannot refuse to give as much help as we can to people who need help. People come to us. Not many. A few. We have friends. We have begged our friends for help for the people who desperately need help. In a few instances, we have been able to get people to safety. Occasionally, we hide someone in our house for a short time. So we have listened to eyewitnesses to what is happening. It is far worse than even we could have imagined."

"But not worse than *I* could have imagined," said Vicky.

"Worse than that," said Gertrude Stein. "I know what you have suffered. It is worse than that."

"Mass murder," said Alice B. Toklas.

"In Poland," said Gertrude Stein, "they started by killing everyone they thought might become focal points for Polish resistance. Political leaders. Military officers. Teachers. University professors. Lawyers. They took them to prisons and shot them. Now they have begun the mass extermination of Jews. They are shooting them down by the hundreds, every day."

"In the Warsaw ghetto?" Vicky asked.

"The Warsaw ghetto is walled in now. The Jews who live there have not enough of anything: shelter, clothing, even water, not to mention food and medicine and decent sanitation. Even so, the ghetto is benevolence compared to what is happening in the countryside."

"Tell every detail," said Alice B. Toklas.

"A German told us this," said Gertrude Stein. "It is why some of them, even from the SS, are shocked and disgusted and sick—and ready to rid themselves of Hitler by whatever means. He was a young lieutenant of the regular army, the *Wehrmacht*. He witnessed a mass execution. Three hundred people, he thinks. That's his estimate. They were brought to a woods, where broad, deep ditches had already been scraped out by machinery. The people were unloaded from trucks and led toward the ditches: men, women, children, infants in arms, old people, young, all of them stark naked. Twenty-five or thirty were prodded forward with bayonets and made to stand at the edge of one of the ditches. Then the SS troops fired on them, and they tumbled into the ditch. Many weren't dead, were screaming, writhing. The troops stepped up to the edge of the ditch and fired down on them, till all were silent."

Gertrude Stein paused for a moment, to recover her voice. "Then they did the same thing again. And again. And again. Until they had shot all the people. Then machines pushed the earth in on top of them. The lieutenant was sure some were still alive and were buried alive. It was not, he told us, an isolated incident. They are doing it every day, all over Poland."

"All Jews?" Vicky asked.

Gertrude Stein nodded. "He thinks so. And not just Polish Jews, either, probably. German Jews. Dutch Jews. French Jews. Taken to Poland, not for resettlement as they say, but to be murdered."

Mrs. Roosevelt had covered her lower face with her hands and had closed her eyes. Now she dropped her hands and shook her head. "What purpose can they possibly think they are serving?" she asked. "When the world finds out, *everyone* will fight them!"

"Do you really feel certain of that?" Vicky asked bitterly.

"They count on the world not finding out," said Gertrude Stein. "But the world must. The lieutenant told us that the SS men stood around chatting and smoking while others prodded the people up to the edges of the pits, and some of them had little cameras and took pictures—particularly when naked girls and women were going by. They took snapshots of them! They also took snapshots of the heaped bodies! Someone must get hands on some of that film!"

Mrs. Roosevelt opened the door into the hall to glance up and down before sending Gertrude Stein and Alice B. Toklas back to their wing of the château.

Haumpsturmführer Giesel came trotting toward her. He gestured that she should get back inside, and he came into the room and closed the door. *"Teufel noch einmal!"* he grunted. *"Die Gestapo kommt!"*

"Warum?" asked Vicky. Why?

"Eine Jude," he said. Looking at Sarah Churchill and seeing she found difficulty following this quick exchange, Giesel switched to English. "A Jew-girl. She evaded the transport last week. She— Who are these women? Huh? Who— Never mind, I know. Stein and Toklas. *Obersturmbannführer* Brandt arranged this. Anyway, eight men are here. Two Gestapo, six SS men. They want this girl. Jeanine Charlet. If they don't find her, they will search the château. I've warned General Rommel and General Rousseau. But there is no place to hide, except in their rooms. Even if we could move

them, we couldn't move their belongings fast enough. We can't have them searching the château! The girl must be turned over to them."

"I don't think they'll find her," said Vicky. "She feared this and fled."

"They will search."

"Do they outrank you, *Herr Hauptsturmführer?*" Vicky sneered. "Do they outrank *Obersturmbannführer* Brandt? You are his deputy, are you not?"

"You would risk us all for this one Jew-girl?"

"I might if I knew where she is," said Vicky. "Fortunately, I don't."

"Fortunately?"

"Yes, fortunately. If they find her, they'll interrogate her. Strenuously. Do you think she could keep our secret?"

"I think you had better use your authority, *Herr Hauptsturmführer,*" said Mrs. Roosevelt.

Giesel stalked out of the room. They heard his boots banging on the floor as he stamped down the hallway to the stairs.

"What can we do?" asked Sarah.

Mrs. Roosevelt shook her head. "Hope he has courage. And can bluff."

"Where is Brandt?" asked Sarah. "We need him. He's the key to the whole damned thing. We need *Obersturmbannführer* Brandt!"

VICKY FOLLOWED GIESEL, KEEPING back far enough that he would not know. She reached inside her dress and checked her pistol. It was there. She would draw it if she needed it.

She could almost read the man's mood from his stride. Stalking along the hall and down the stairs, he had been angry. Now, on the stone floors below, his footsteps did not echo so loud—not so fast or firm. He was having second thoughts, she judged. Then he strode faster, and by the time he reached the door and walked toward the bridge, he was stamping again. Determination. He was, after all, what she had reminded him: *Hauptsturmführer* of the *Sicherheitsdienst;* and the SD was the elite corps of the SS, answerable only to Heydrich or Himmler—and not to Müller of the Gestapo.

A man in a raincoat was the apparent leader of the squad of eight coming through the gate. Vivienne Duval had delayed them a few minutes at the bridge, but they had brushed by her now and entered the château. A second man also wore a raincoat. The six others were in the black uniform of the SS. Two of them carried submachine guns.

Vicky crouched in a doorway and listened.

* * *

She did not know someone else was listening. Kevin O'Neil, standing just inside a window he had just opened, in the bedroom where Brandt had been killed, gripped the Schmeisser submachine gun from under his bed, listened to the talk below, and gauged his chances of knocking down all eight men with one 32-round burst. If this was the fatal invasion of the château, the only chance for escape would be to eliminate this squad. Others would come, but they wouldn't arrive for half an hour anyway.

What was more, if he decided to fire, would he take down *Hauptsturmführer* Giesel while he was at it? Which side would Giesel be on after he saw eight SS and Gestapo men shot down?

Kevin sighted the Schmeisser on the Germans, noted with gratitude that the uniformed men were not spreading out, and strained to listen to the talk.

The talk was in German—

"Herr Hauptsturmführer. Is *Obersturmbannführer* Brandt here?"

"No. He is away from here at the moment. He left me in charge."

"When did you last see him?"

Giesel shrugged. "An hour ago. Half an hour ago. Why do you ask?"

"For no reason," said the leading Gestapo man. "We thought we would see him here. His office believes he is here."

"So he is. Or was. Your name is—?"

"Kriminalinspektor Schillings, *Herr Hauptsturmführer."*

Giesel nodded curtly. He made a dramatic point of glancing past Schillings, at the armed SS men. "Were you informed, *Herr Kriminalinspektor,* that a secret conference is being held in this château?"

"We have come only to arrest one of the servants, *Herr Hauptsturmführer.* A Jew."

"Name this Jew, and he will be delivered to you."

"The Jew is a woman," said Schillings. "She was overlooked

in Friday's roundup of Jew spies, because she had taken employment here and was not to be found in any of the Jew-sites."

"Her name?"

"Jeanine Charlet, *Herr Hauptsturmführer.*"

"I will have her brought out, if she is here. Now— Order your men to wait outside."

"My orders are to search for her."

Giesel raised his chin high. "Indeed? Did anyone tell you what is going on here? I will trust you far enough to tell you, *Herr Kriminalinspektor.* The word must go no further."

Schillings nodded.

"*Eine Führerschaftkonferenz,*" said Giesel. A leadership conference. "I have said too much."

Schillings nodded curtly. "Very well, *Herr Hauptsturmführer.* You will deliver the Jew-girl?"

"If we can find her," said Giesel.

Vicky sprinted through the halls and across the courtyard toward the kitchen. She burst into the kitchen, where Jeanine sat placidly peeling apples. The only other woman in the kitchen was the cook, a pallid older woman.

"Gestapo! Here to arrest you, Jeanine!"

The girl sprang to her feet.

"I told them you left here a long time ago."

Jeanine turned and stared at the cook. "*Madame . . . ?*"

Vicky spoke to the cook. "If they take her, she'll die."

The cook glanced back and forth between them. "Then *go!*" she snapped.

Vicky led Jeanine from the kitchen, through a pantry, and down a corridor toward the stable. "Hide for a while," she said. "Then we'll get you out of here."

As Kevin watched, Vivienne Duval accompanied Giesel through the gate and across the bridge, to where the Gestapo and SS men waited. He couldn't hear what they said. He knew he could chop them down as they came through the gate and hoped Madame Duval would walk a little apart.

But after a few minutes, Giesel and Madame Duval returned alone. The Germans outside mounted their vehicles and drove away.

"For the moment," said Giesel a few minutes later in Mrs. Roosevelt's room. "For the moment, they are gone. They accepted my word that the Jew-girl ran away this morning. They accepted my word that a secret conference is being held here. I am certain, just the same, that they will report the matter to Paris, maybe to Berlin. And then what?"

Kevin strolled into the room just in time to hear Giesel's last words. "We are safe, my friend," he said insouciantly. "This is Friday afternoon, soon Friday evening. Even at the *Reichssicherheitshauptamt*, a weekend is beginning. Reports arriving this evening will not get much attention before Monday morning—particularly if they involve nothing more than the inability of your chums to add one more Jew to the twelve thousand they arrested *last* Friday."

"Where is Vicky?" asked Mrs. Roosevelt.

Vicky was with General Rousseau and Gabrielle, telling them essentially the same thing that Kevin was saying: that the intrusion of the Gestapo and SS had been part of an effort to find a young Jewish woman who had escaped their roundup of last Friday and had nothing to do with the conference.

"If we've been betrayed, we've been betrayed," she said. "It's too late to run."

General Rousseau agreed. "I will say the same to General Rommel."

"The conference will begin again over dinner, if this is agreeable, *Monsieur le Général*. I believe a little entertainment has been arranged for later."

Gabrielle smiled. "I can assure *le Général* of that," she said.

* * *

Mrs. Roosevelt met in her room with Vicky and Kevin. It was time, she said, for them to evaluate the situation.

"What we have come here to do does not seem impossible," she said to begin the meeting. "We have taken risks. We are asked to take more. The risks are justified. I am not happy with all the things I hear the generals talking about, but if their conversations result in the removal of Herr Hitler from power and a truce, tens of thousands of lives—and maybe more—may be saved."

"The question," said Vicky, "is whether or not the death of Brandt leaves the generals with no realistic way of ridding the world of Adolf Hitler. Does Giesel really know what Brandt planned? I doubt it. And we can't ask him, can we?"

"I am not so sure," said Mrs. Roosevelt. "Maybe that is precisely what we should do. He seems to be forthcoming, as was Colonel Brandt."

"Rommel seems to accept him," said Kevin.

"Another question," said Mrs. Roosevelt. "We have not taken Miss Churchill—Mrs. Oliver—into our confidence at all. Should we?"

"When we must," said Vicky. "Not until."

"Everything," said Kevin, "depends on who killed Brandt. I can't see that we're makin' any progress toward findin' out."

"A thought has come to my mind," said the First Lady. "I've been reviewing the facts, over and over, in my mind, looking for something suggestive. I have a question, Vicky. Last night you and Jeanine drove Colonel Brandt's car away. Did you switch on the headlights before you left the grounds of the château?"

"Of course not," said Vicky. "We didn't switch them on at all. We drove without lights. We didn't dare turn them on."

"I suspected as much," said Mrs. Roosevelt. "On the terrace, Madame Duval told us she was wakened this morning by the headlights of a car, flashing on the curtains of her window. But what car was that? Was there another parked nearby when you and Jeanine left in Colonel Brandt's car?"

"No."

"Then—"

"Then either another car left earlier," said Vicky, "or came and left later, or—"

"Or Madame Duval is lying," said Kevin.

"I should not want to jump to *that* conclusion," said Mrs. Roosevelt. "But I believe we would agree that relatively few automobiles are moving on the roads of France these days, particularly in the hours between midnight and dawn. This car—"

"May have carried the killer," said Vicky.

"Or killers," said Kevin.

"Or Madame Duval is not telling the truth," said Mrs. Roosevelt. "I should very much like to know who was driving that car."

Madame Vivienne Duval knocked on the door and was admitted to Mrs. Roosevelt's room immediately after Kevin O'Neil left. It was as though she had been waiting, watching for him to leave.

She sat down without being asked to. "We have a thing or two to discuss," she said in English.

"I'll leave, Madame," said Vicky quietly, playing the role of maid.

"Please stay. You are what I want to talk about."

"Miss Klein is—" Mrs. Roosevelt began.

"Dear lady!" Vivienne Duval interrupted. "Everything we care for is at stake. Our lives are at stake. Our chances diminish with every lie we tell each other."

"Lies . . . ?"

Vivienne Duval stared hard at Vicky. "A lady's maid! I'd sooner believe she is an American Baptist evangelist. No. She is an intelligence agent. Someone's. Nearly everyone here is. What is more, everyone knows it. Including *Hauptsturmführer* Giesel. I suggest we drop the pretense."

"Let's continue it," said Vicky. "It may yet prove useful."

"Giesel knows?" asked Mrs. Roosevelt. "How does he know?"

"*Fräulein* Viktoria Neustadt is the subject of an extensive dossier in Vichy Gestapo headquarters," said Vivienne Duval. "That dossier was brought here after she was identified as having escaped from Austria into France and as having become active in the *Résistance*—in the *Maquis*, actually: the armed guerrilla bands of the *Résistance*. That she remains alive here is ample evidence of the good faith of *Obersturmbannführer* Brandt and *Hauptsturmführer* Giesel."

"You seem to know a great deal, Madame," said Vicky.

"When I agreed to lend this house for the conference, I insisted on knowing who would be here," said Vivienne Duval. "Where, incidentally, *Fräulein*, is the body of the *Obersturmbannführer*?"

"Body . . . ?" asked Mrs. Roosevelt.

"Don't you know?" asked Vivienne Duval. "Brandt is dead. Murdered. In his room last night."

"What makes you think so?" asked Vicky aggressively.

Vivienne Duval tossed her head and smirked. "A man hardly lies on his face on the floor of his room, with a bullet hole in the back of his head, if he was *not* murdered," she said.

"You saw the body?" asked Mrs. Roosevelt.

"It's my house. I know the creaks in the night. I know the sound of a shot. I went to his room. I saw the body. I waited for a time, to be sure everyone along that hallway was asleep, and then I came back with two trusted servants to remove the body. It was gone. So was the blood-soaked rug where he had been lying. So was part of his luggage." She turned to Vicky. "You were not in your room. I had my two men check when they went back to the servants' wing. Neither was Jeanine Charlet. If you killed *Obersturmbannführer* Brandt, or if friends of yours did it, you have jeopardized everything this conference was called to accomplish—not to mention all our lives."

"I didn't kill him," said Vicky. "And I don't know who did."

"Well, I can't cross-examine you. But I am anxious to know what is going on."

"What are you suggesting?" asked Mrs. Roosevelt.

"I am suggesting," said Vivienne Duval, "that someone acting on motives very different from yours and mine murdered *Obersturmbannführer* Brandt. I am suggesting that we had better manage to keep that a secret until the conspiracy here being negotiated becomes a reality and produces results. Otherwise—" Like most French people, she was skilled at the Gallic shrug. "Where is the body? If it remains in the château, it had better be cleverly hidden. And where, I must also ask, is Jeanine Charlet?"

"Still here in the château, Madame," said Vicky. "Will *Hauptsturmführer* Giesel cooperate so fully as to help her escape from here?"

"To go where?"

"Maybe *he* has an idea."

Vivienne Duval smiled cynically. "Yes, I am sure. Go and speak to her, *Fräulein*. Tell her she will have help."

Vicky nodded and left the room.

"You could be served by a less conspicuous aide," said Vivienne Duval. "Before *Obersturmbannführer* Brandt would agree to participate in this meeting, he insisted on knowing exactly who would be here. He was astounded to learn that a woman wanted by the Gestapo would be coming with you."

"General Rousseau trusts her," said Mrs. Roosevelt. "I believe that is the point. General Rousseau wanted me to be served and to some degree protected by a person he knows and trusts."

"She may have killed *Obersturmbannführer* Brandt, you know," said Vivienne Duval. "She is from Vienna. He was in Vienna as an SD officer. They may have met there. Or she may have blamed him for what happened to her parents and brother."

"I am aware of the possibility," said Mrs. Roosevelt.

"May I suggest," said Vivienne Duval, "that you don't tell anyone Brandt is dead. I mean, of course, Miss Churchill. Obviously the generals don't know and must not be told. They are making good progress, aren't they?"

Mrs. Roosevelt nodded. "It's like a Congress of Vienna with

only two representatives. They sit there calmly dividing up Europe—"

"If their division ends the war, achieves the liberation of France, secures the return of prisoners . . . Let them divide Europe any way they want to."

"I wonder about their authority," said Mrs. Roosevelt. "Whom do they represent? Will General de Gaulle, for example, accept what General Rousseau agrees to? Even if Hitler is overthrown, will the new leaders carry out an agreement negotiated by General Rommel?"

"*Obersturmbannführer* Brandt was confident about the German side. He said Göring did not want to go to war in 1939 and emphatically does not want to invade Russia. Most of the generals feel the same way. He felt certain that a quick, successful *coup d'état* will put Hitler aside, dead or alive, and leave power in the hands of those who are anxious for a negotiated peace."

"I hope the loss of Colonel Brandt does not spoil everything," said Mrs. Roosevelt.

"Let us so pray," said Vivienne Duval.

The rain had stopped, and the dinner hour began with cocktails and champagne on the terrace. The two generals were in an affable mood. Rommel especially seemed to have relaxed several degrees. He sat on the stone balustrade, sipping champagne, chatting with Gabrielle. His *Pour le Mérite* glittered in the sunlight. Kevin stood a little apart with *Hauptsturmführer* Giesel, talking with him. Mrs. Roosevelt guessed Kevin was trying to pump the German a little, to see what he could find out. Sarah Churchill all but monopolized the attention of the First Lady. She talked about the Blitz, describing London landmarks that Mrs. Roosevelt knew, that had been obliterated by the bombs.

"Does it bother you that the *Obersturmbannführer* has not come back?" Kevin asked Giesel. Their conversation was in German.

Giesel nodded. "I can't imagine where he could be."

"May we assume that he is somewhere pursuing our common purpose?"

"Yes, I suppose so," said Giesel.

"Without asking you to name anyone," said Kevin, "I would like to ask if you and he were the only SD or SS officers who know what is going on here."

"There are . . . others."

"In Vichy?"

"Yes. And in Berlin."

"Not, I should imagine, *Kriminalinspektor* Schillings."

Giesel shook his head. "No."

"Is there any possibility that *Obersturmbannführer* Brandt has been arrested?"

"May God forbid!" muttered Giesel.

Two toasts exchanged at the dinner table were a surprise.

Rommel rose first. Bowing slightly to General Rousseau, he raised his glass and said, *"A l'honneur de la France!"*

The French general then rose. His lips twitched under his great mustache. He seemed overcome with emotion, and he hesitated for a moment. *"A l'honneur d'une Allemagne nouvelle!"*

At the end of the dinner Vivienne Duval rose. "We have arranged for a bit of entertainment this evening," she said. "I have observed that the conversations have gone well, so perhaps it is not essential that every moment be given to negotiating. A very famous entertainer is living in southern France, and *Obersturmbannführer* Brandt made it possible for her to come here this evening. May I present Miss Josephine Baker!"

Mrs. Roosevelt could not have been more surprised. She knew Josephine Baker, whom she had met on an Atlantic crossing aboard the *Normandie* in 1938. It was no exaggeration to say they had become friends. She knew Miss Baker was a French citizen, by marriage; and she knew the beloved entertainer had refused to leave France in 1940 and had only moved to the south. It was an act of great courage, since hers was perhaps the most recognizable face in France and since Nazi race policy might cause her to be shamefully abused.

A trio of musicians entered the dining room and took chairs placed for them beyond the head of the table. They began to play: lively jazz, on a clarinet, a saxophone, and a guitar.

The petite and elegant star entered. She wore a simple white dress that contrasted dramatically with her *café-au-lait* complexion. Her black hair was close-cut and slicked down in the style Frenchwomen had tried to imitate in what had been called *baker-fixer les cheveux*—to fix the hair in the Baker style. She was unique. She was talented.

For twenty minutes, just that and no more, Josephine Baker sang and danced for the dinner guests. Though Mrs. Roosevelt had met her and thought she knew her, she had never seen a Baker performance. She understood, now, why France loved Josephine Baker.

La Baker, as the French called her—or *la Joséphine terrible*—was thirty-five years old but still as vivacious and exuberant as she had been when, at nineteen, she had first appeared on the Paris stage.

General Rommel rose to his feet when she finished and was taking her bows. He reached behind him and drew a chair to the table. *"Mademoiselle, s'il vous plaît,"* he said.

She hesitated for an instant, then smiled and took the chair beside him. *"Monsieur le Général,"* she murmured.

Rommel's French was spare and awkward, but he told her he regretted his duties had so long prevented him seeing her perform—since he had heard her name and had been curious about her, for many years.

The contrast was dazzling: stiff German general who could not entirely relax, no matter how hard he tried, and gamine American star who would have been unable, probably, to be entirely somber, no matter how hard she tried, uniformed representative of stiff German militarism and a grotesquely racist regime, and

daughter of a black woman from St. Louis, Missouri, and a Span-
iard whose lofty family had prevented Josephine's mother and father from marrying.

Rommel offered her champagne, and she sat and drank with
him, also eating delicacies he offered her from the serving plates
that remained on the table. Doubtless it was a night both of them
would remember.

Mrs. Roosevelt could not imagine why Josephine Baker was
here. That she had come to entertain the two generals, the American First Lady, and the daughter of the British prime minister was
not a reasonable explanation.

It was not the explanation, either.

After midnight, when the generals were in their bedrooms,
Josephine Baker sat on the terrace overlooking the formal garden
of the château, in the fragrant warmth of a summer night. She
sipped champagne. Mrs. Roosevelt joined her in champagne, as did
Sarah Churchill and Vivienne Duval. Vicky and Kevin drank whiskey.

Josephine had changed from her white dress and now wore a
loose-fitting khaki tunic and pants.

"The invasion of Russia may be coming sooner than we
thought," said Josephine. "The urgency is even greater. The generals must signal they have come to an agreement. As soon as possible."

"What is the source of this information?" asked Mrs. Roosevelt.

"I thought you'd been told," said Josephine. She glanced
around. "Since the lives of all of us here are equally at risk, I suppose we must trust each other. I thought you'd been told that I act
as a liaison between the *Résistance* and British Intelligence."

"*I* was told," said Sarah Churchill.

"I didn't come here to sing songs and dance," said Josephine.
"Or to make friends with the Desert Fox, charming man though he
is."

"Charming and naive," said Vicky. "Politically naive."

"If there were a free election in Germany today, he could be elected president," said Kevin.

"But there is not going to be a free election," said Vicky.

I have something more important to talk about," said Vivienne Duval. "Does anyone in the *Résistance* know what has become of *Obersturmbannführer* Brandt?"

"No one has mentioned him," said Josephine.

"You know who I mean?"

"I have heard the name. I don't know who he is, precisely, or why you ask."

"Why are you here, actually, Miss Baker?" asked Mrs. Roosevelt.

"Mid-conference contact," said Josephine. "They don't want you using your radio unless it's absolutely necessary. Their word to you is: *faster, faster!* They would like a progress report."

"The two generals are dividing up Europe like two kids dividing their toys," said Sarah Churchill.

"Beyond that, there is a problem," said Vivienne Duval. "The representative of the German . . . How shall we call them? Security services? *Obersturmbannführer* Brandt. He is missing. He was here yesterday. Last night—"

"We have to tell the truth," said Mrs. Roosevelt grimly. "Last night he was murdered. Shot in the back of the head."

"Who did it?" asked Josephine.

"You've kept this from me!" protested Sarah Churchill.

"The generals don't know," said Mrs. Roosevelt, glancing at Sarah and returning her focus to Josephine Baker. *"Hauptsturmführer* Giesel doesn't know."

Josephine shook her head. "I don't know what all this means. I wasn't given all the information."

"Give the word to your contact," said Mrs. Roosevelt. "They may decide the whole scheme has been lost."

"But who killed him? Don't you have any idea?"

"It was professionally done," said Vicky. "Silenced pistol. I think he may have been compromised, and someone came here and killed him."

"We're *all* compromised if that is true," said Sarah.

"*Hauptsturmführer* Giesel," said Vicky. "Has it occurred to anyone that he might have entered the château last night and—"

"Then why are we all sitting here, not arrested, not yet interfered with?" asked Vivienne Duval.

"Too many prominent people involved," said Vicky. "They really don't want to arrest Mrs. Roosevelt. Or Sarah Churchill. Not to mention General Rommel and General Rousseau. But when the famous people are gone . . ."

"What a coup, if they did it," said Kevin. "Then they could sort us all out: some to the wall, some to the camps, some to the border."

"*Where is the body?*" Vivienne Duval asked in a shrill, angry whisper. "I don't think Giesel carried it out."

"You assume he acted alone," said Vicky.

"A question for your liaison contact, Miss Baker," said Mrs. Roosevelt. "Did someone of the *Résistance* kill Colonel Brandt? If so, did they know what they were doing?"

"I won't have time to ask," said Josephine. "That is, to ask and return an answer. The other question I am to ask is—when do you want to leave here? I understand there are alternatives A, B, and C. I only want to know which alternative you choose."

Mrs. Roosevelt looked to Kevin, then to Vicky. "I believe we should choose alternative A," she said. "Do you agree?"

Vicky nodded. "If we have to change it, we can use the radio."

Alternative A meant they would leave Montrond on Sunday afternoon. This was after midnight on Friday, and it was the First Lady's judgment that anything they were going to accomplish they would accomplish tomorrow. Likely they would leave without knowing who killed Brandt. What was far more important, they would leave after seeing the two generals reach an agreement that might—might, somehow, if great good fortune prevailed—be carried into effect and establish an uneasy truce in Europe. After tomorrow, Saturday, it was not likely anything more would be accomplished.

"Send back word," said Mrs. Roosevelt, "that this mission seems to have been worthwhile."

"I will do that," said Josephine Baker solemnly.

"Are you certain, my dear," asked the First Lady, "that you would not like to join us as we leave France? There will be room for another person."

Josephine rose from her chair and came to take Mrs. Roosevelt's hand. "Thank you," she whispered. "But *vive la France!* This country has been good to me. I will serve it."

Josephine Baker and her musicians slipped away from Montrond as inconspicuously as they had come, just after two A.M.

Vivienne Duval asked Mrs. Roosevelt to remain on the terrace and speak with her alone after all the others had left. She poured the last of a bottle of champagne into her own glass, after the First Lady had shaken her head at the offer of more.

"You must forgive me," said Vivienne Duval in French. "As *châtelaine* of Montrond, I have keys to all rooms. I have prowled about a good deal. I have violated *your* privacy. I know, for example, that you have possession, now, of certain papers and scrapbooks of *Obersturmbannführer* Brandt." She shrugged. "I don't care about that. I know who he was. But there is something I think you should know."

"I shall be happy to know everything I can," said Mrs. Roosevelt.

"I have searched the rooms of your Mr. O'Neil. Rather ordinary man, if his possessions are evidence. But he has in his rooms two things I think you should know about."

"Which are?"

"One, a Schmeisser submachine gun. May I suggest to you that I don't think he was carrying it when he came here? A Schmeisser does not fold up and fit in someone's luggage. That means he has a contact here. Maybe you know who it is."

"I don't," said Mrs. Roosevelt.

"A lesser point," said Vivienne Duval. "It could have been given him by the *Maquis*, by the SD, or—or by someone working with him on private motives. But it's still a minor point."

"The major point, then, please," said Mrs. Roosevelt.

"In a leather bag, under his bed with the submachine gun, your Mr. O'Neil is carrying a very substantial amount of money in Swiss gold francs. I couldn't count it, but I would estimate it as something like fifty thousand gold francs. Do you have any idea why he would be carrying *that* with him? Does anything you are doing here imply paying someone fifty thousand gold francs?"

"Describe the bag," said Mrs. Roosevelt.

"Black leather. A valise. Like a doctor's bag."

"Yes. Well . . . I don't know," said Mrs. Roosevelt.

She knew he hadn't been carrying it when they left the *Skip-jack*, hadn't been carrying it when they arrived at Montrond.

IX

MRS. ROOSEVELT HAD BEEN in her room no more than three-quarters of an hour after she left Vivienne Duval on the terrace. She had spent a little time washing and combing her hair, and was reading in *Obersturmbannführer* Brandt's files when she heard the rap on her door.

She opened the door. Vivienne Duval.

"There has been another murder," whispered the terrified woman.

"Who?"

"I don't even know. The body lies in the hall."

The First Lady pulled on a dressing gown and followed Vivienne along the hallway. Dawn was no more than half an hour away, the sky was milky gray, and faint light entered the hall from the big windows at both ends. In that light Mrs. Roosevelt could make out the form lying on the floor outside the room occupied by General Rommel. Thank God it was not the general.

"I touched him," whispered Vivienne Duval. "He's dead . . ."

Mrs. Roosevelt glanced up and down the hall. "He wasn't here when we came upstairs."

"No."

"Do you recognize him?"

"Not that way."

The body lay face down. In the dim light they could not see what had killed the man.

Lying beside him on the floor was some sort of tool that Mrs. Roosevelt did not recognize.

Mrs. Roosevelt stared along the hallway, first one way and then the other. "We can't leave him here," she said. "The generals must not know. Giesel must not know."

Vivienne Duval turned decisively toward the door to the room where Brandt had been killed. Selecting a key from a key ring that hung from her belt, she unlocked and opened the door. The two women grabbed the body by the legs and dragged it across the hall and into the room.

Vivienne closed the door and turned on the light. She knelt and turned the body over.

"I don't know him," she whispered.

Mrs. Roosevelt knelt. "I don't see what killed him," she said. Then, after a moment, she did see what had killed him. At the back of his head, where the spine meets the skull, the skull was caved in, as by a powerful blow. The depression in the skull was not broad, but it was deep. The blow that had made it had crushed bone into brain, but the skin was only minimally broken, and but little blood had oozed from the wound.

The man was bigger than average: taller and heavier. He was dressed in rough, serviceable civilian clothes, including rubber boots of the kind worn by farmers in this part of France. His eyes were open, with an expression as if of astonishment. His hair was light, the eyes blue. He had not shaved today.

"You have no idea who he might be?"

Vivienne Duval shook her head.

Mrs. Roosevelt drew a deep breath and glanced around the room as if she expected to discover something else surprising. "I think we have to take Kevin O'Neil into our confidence. Also, *Fräulein* Neustadt—Vicky."

Vivienne stood. "You trust that one more than I do. You ignore my warnings about her."

"We have to trust her," said Mrs. Roosevelt. "As we do Kevin. They know everything."

"We have to trust each other," Vivienne added.

Mrs. Roosevelt nodded. "I will go and fetch Vicky. Will you go for Kevin?"

"Yes. Do you know where the *Fräulein's* room is? In the servants' wing . . ."

"Yes. I went to see it, shortly after we arrived."

Vivienne smiled wryly. "You take care of your people, don't you?"

Mrs. Roosevelt returned to her room and dressed in her khaki skirt and jacket, with a white cotton blouse. She walked across the inner courtyard of the château as the sky began to show red. The servants' wing was to the rear of Montrond—that is, on the side away from the river, the side where the stable was located, and the kitchen and pantry. The rooms provided for the household staff were small and modest, yet cozy—at least Vicky's was. She knocked lightly on the door. When she heard no response, she knocked more firmly. Still nothing from within. She tried the door. It was unlocked. She opened it and looked in.

Vicky was not there.

In Brandt's room, Kevin O'Neil knelt beside the body of the unidentified man and went through his pockets.

"Interestin'," he said to Mrs. Roosevelt as she came in. "No identification. Nowt. Y' don't wander about in this part of th' world in these times with no papers on y'r person. Which means . . . It means this man came here to do no good."

"I judge that assumption to be really a bit facile," said Mrs. Roosevelt.

"Th' tool y' found beside him. What do y' think that is? I'll tell you. It's a picklock, made for pryin' open the simple kind of old locks they've got on the doors in the château."

The First Lady nodded. "Suggestive evidence," she said.

"Here's somethin' that will maybe convince y'," said Kevin. He had felt the man's pockets and now reached in and pulled from the right-hand jacket pocket a small black pistol.

Vivienne's mouth dropped open, and she stared wide-eyed at the little weapon.

"Well, then . . ." said Kevin, scowling over the pistol. "This may answer a question. It's a Beretta. Italian manufacture. But look at this." He pulled the slide, and one of the cartridges was expelled. He picked it up from the floor. "That's what you call a twenty-two caliber long rifle cartridge. It's also what you call a hollow-point cartridge. A little pistol like this doesn't make much noise when it's fired. But drivin' a twenty-two hollow-point into the back of a man's head would put a sure end to him. I may have been wrong when I said nine millimeter."

"Are you suggesting this man may have killed Colonel Brandt?" asked Mrs. Roosevelt.

"Couldn't say. There's more than one twenty-two pistol in the world. They're common as old shoes. I'm sayin' it's possible. What was he doin' here tonight?"

"A better question. Who killed him?"

"A very good question. The answer to my question is probably also the answer to yours. If we knew what th' man was doin' here, we would probably know who killed him, and why."

Vivienne Duval had sat down. "I regret I ever agreed to allow this meeting to be held here," she said. "All I want is to live here quietly until the war ends and the Germans leave—if they ever do. My chances of living here, quietly or otherwise, diminish hourly.

"How did it happen that the meeting was arranged for here?" asked Mrs. Roosevelt. "That was never explained to me."

"*Obersturmbannführer* Brandt came to me a month or so ago and proposed it. At first he did not hint at how important the meeting would be, only said that it would be secret and that for the meeting he would stock the château with an abundance of food and wine. I accepted the proposal on that basis—though, of course, my enthusiasm for it would have been a thousand times greater if I'd had any idea who was meeting and why."

"You knew Colonel Brandt before, then?"

"Mrs. Roosevelt," said Vivienne severely, "you must face the fact that Artur Brandt was no colonel, though I know he introduced himself to you as a colonel. He never served in the German army. He was an *Obersturmbannführer* SS. Worse than that, he was an officer of the *Sicherheitsdienst*, which is the Gestapo of the Gestapo."

"And so is *Hauptsturmführer* Giesel," said Mrs. Roosevelt. "I dislike twisting my tongue around these grotesque, arrogant titles."

"When did you first meet *Obersturmbannführer* Brandt?" asked Kevin.

"Shortly after he arrived in Vichy," said Vivienne. "Nine or ten months ago."

"In what circumstance?" asked Mrs. Roosevelt.

"I think I was very fortunate that my home—it is my father's home, actually—was not seized as SD headquarters. I think it would have been if it had been a little closer to Vichy. Anyway . . . He came back from time to time. He liked Montrond. I suspected he was thinking about taking it for his personal residence."

Kevin glanced toward the window. The curtains were closed, but the sunlight behind them was evident. "Daylight," he said. "We can't put this one down the well."

"Wrap him in something and slide him under the bed," said Vivienne. "The conference ends today. Tomorrow everyone will be gone. I will take care of him then."

"If we are lucky," said Kevin. "I've got a feelin' the man had friends. And enemies. Someone will be missin' him. For sure. I'll be curious to know who asks after him."

"I should be curious," said Mrs. Roosevelt to Kevin when she was alone with him in the hall, "to know where Vicky is."

Kevin nodded. "We've got two or three hours before th' generals come down for breakfast," he said. "Have y' had any sleep?"

"Who could sleep?"

"Well . . . Me neither, now, I guess. Let's go see if there's any coffee to be had."

They walked together to the kitchen, checking Vicky's room again and finding her still not there. Though aware that coffee was a scarce commodity in this time and place, they explored the kitchen, found coffee, and Kevin set to work to brew a pot.

The kitchen of the château was a traditional French Provincial kitchen, made large. Heavy old copper pots hung from the ceiling. In days before the food shortages of 1941 it had undoubtedly been hung with garlic and dried tomatoes.

"Felled by a very hard blow to the back of the head," said Mrs. Roosevelt.

"Not necessarily so hard," he said. "Delivered with something heavy. Hard . . . heavy. Same result."

"In other words, a woman could have struck the blow."

Kevin nodded. "Y'r mind works the same way as y'rs truly's does."

"Vicky?"

"Or Vivienne. Or Jeanine. Or Gabrielle."

"Of course it was not *necessarily* a woman."

Kevin grinned. "No. Not necessarily."

Mrs. Roosevelt sat at the kitchen table, on a sturdy wooden chair, and was conscious of the red light of dawn that gradually filled the room. Looking around at the solid room with all its solid fixtures, she was moved to a fondness for the place; and she found herself thinking of the generations of people who had worked here, the other generations who had been served from here. She'd had little time during her stay to appreciate the history and beauty of Montrond; but now, for a moment, appreciation flooded over her.

What a simplicity of life this kitchen represented—and what a complexity and sophistication, the grand rooms of the château! King Francis II had visited here, almost certainly. And Henri IV. Probably Louis XIV. Maybe Napoleon.

"The coffee will be ready shortly," said Kevin, breaking into a reverie he had detected. "Allow me to remind you of something, if I may. Dear lady, we are under no obligation to try to find out who killed *Obersturmbannführer* Brandt and the man under the bed upstairs. What we must do is get away from here, having done what we came here to accomplish."

"Did someone warn you that I might try to play Sherlock Holmes?" she asked.

He put his big warm hand down on hers. "Now, it was suggested. 'Try t' discourage her,' somebody said, 'from seekin' to solve any crime that might be committed in the neighborhood whilst y're there.' She doesn't like to leave problems unsolved, somebody said."

"My husband is a witty man."

"I've not met y'r husband. I think I'd like him. Th' man who married *you* has my respect."

"Kevin—"

"Y've qualities not superficial," he said.

She withdrew her hand from under his. "I would like to know who killed . . . *Obersturmbannführer*"—she forced out the ugly title—"Brandt. No. Let me correct the statement. I am not so much interested in *who* killed him as in *why*. The result of this conference—plus our chances of escaping from here—may well depend on *why*."

"Well said. Also, I'd like to know who we have hidden under th' bed. But if we get away from here and return home without ever findin' out, I think we will both be satisfied."

The coffee was ready, and Kevin poured two cups. He did not offer to search for cream or sugar. The coffee he had made was deadly black and strong.

"Saturday," said Mrs. Roosevelt as she took a cautious sip and winced at its heat and strength. "June 21, 1941. Who could believe we are here? Trying to encourage peace for the world and confronted with two murders in two nights."

"Executions, perhaps," Kevin suggested.

"Another word for murder, very often," she said.

"I—"

He stopped. Jeanine Charlet came into the kitchen. Looking sleepy, like a young woman who had just forced herself to leave her bed, she stopped in the doorway and stared at Mrs. Roosevelt and Kevin O'Neil.

Mrs. Roosevelt was a little distressed to see her. She had wanted to believe that the absence of Vicky would be explained when they learned that Vicky had spent the night helping Jeanine to escape the château and the attentions of the Gestapo.

"Have a cup of coffee," said Kevin, speaking French.

Jeanine tossed her head upward and toward the grand wings of the château. "Soon they may start calling for eggs and coffee and . . . for everything that people outside the château can't have," she said. "Monsieur de Luc, the butler, is in the pantry across, where the speaking tubes sound. The *garçon* will come running, I will have ready, and he will carry to the room."

"What a grossly inefficient way to serve," said Mrs. Roosevelt.

"That occurred to me, too," said Jeanine. "I've not always been a maidservant, you know. In fact . . . I am *not* a maidservant. *Dammit!* I—"

"It is possible," said Mrs. Roosevelt, "that you can accompany us when we leave here. I will take you to the United States."

"Thank you, Madame. I will stay as close as possible to my family."

Mrs. Roosevelt glanced at Kevin. Last night she had offered Josephine Baker a way of leaving France. Now, Jeanine. She meant to offer the same to Gertrude Stein and Alice B. Toklas. Escape from Nazi-dominated . . . But she suspected Gertrude Stein would refuse, too. And Vicky had said she would not leave when their mission was completed.

"Where is Vicky? Do you know?"

Jeanine shook her head. "I haven't seen her since last evening. She sat here in the kitchen and drank brandy for half an hour.

Helping herself to the brandy proved that she is no maidservant."

"Jeanine . . . Could anything bad have happened to Vicky? Don't withhold anything you know."

"You don't need to worry about Vicky," said Jeanine. "She will survive all of us."

"I am not quite sure if that is a compliment to Vicky or—"

"It is a simple statement of fact, Madame," said Jeanine. "Vicky means to survive. *And so do I.*"

"An appropriate sentiment," said Kevin. "The only question is, *how* will you survive? And what will you do to make it possible?"

Jeanine busied herself, jerking boxes from the cabinets, eggs from an icebox where there was no ice. She frowned at the coffee pot. "Will you finish what's in it," she said, "so I can make a big pot for the important people in the other wing?"

Kevin poured coffee into two more cups. "We work together," he said. "You and I and Mrs. Roosevelt are on the same side."

"You are on the side of the Jews?" asked Jeanine skeptically. She turned toward Mrs. Roosevelt and with her eyes repeated the question.

"We are on the side of humanity," said the First Lady solemnly. "There is no Jewish side, or German side, or French side. Or American side. There is the side of life and justice and dignity— and the side of death and injustice and shame. Many Germans are on the first side. Probably some Jews are on the other."

"Do you think so? I am not—"

"*C'est assez!*" snapped Kevin. "We haven't time for a reading of the Declaration of the Rights of Man. Not now. Do you know where Vicky is, or not?"

"I don't know," said Jeanine. "She left here during the night. I do not sleep well. I heard her go out. I don't know what time it was. I don't have a watch or a clock in my room."

"Was it still entirely dark when she left?"

Jeanine nodded.

Mrs. Roosevelt glanced at Kevin. Both of them understood that the young woman may have heard Vicky leaving to come to the two A.M. meeting on the terrace, or may have heard her leaving later.

"Well, I suppose we've no choice but to return to our rooms and try to sleep a little," said the First Lady. "We can't go out searching for Vicky. But please tell her, when she comes in, that I would like to see her."

In her room again, Mrs. Roosevelt found it impossible to sleep. She had been reading in Brandt's files—struggling with the German—when Vivienne Duval came to tell her there was a body lying in the hall. She sat in bed and looked through some more of this paper.

She found nothing to suggest even the possibility that he would turn against Hitler. Well . . . Of course not. He would have carried no incriminating documents. In fact, it was doubtful there *were* documents. No one would dare write out the conspirators' plans.

He had been carrying a thin file on Vivienne Duval—a few documents in French, only one in German. A summary of her husband's army record was there, though with no word either of his capture or of his death.

One of the French documents appeared to be the cover sheet for Vivienne Duval's dossier—a printed form with blanks in which information had been written with pen: her maiden name, married name, date of birth, place of birth, date and place of marriage, and so on. On the line specifying *Nationalité*, someone had written *Française—Juive*.

Attached to that sheet was an identity card bearing her photograph. Information had been written on the card as it had been on the cover sheet. One line was significantly different. For *Nationalité*, the writing said "merely" *Française*.

Mrs. Roosevelt noticed, too—and wondered why—Vivienne had not signed this identity card.

The document in German was a list of about twenty Jews liv-

ing in Fleurs and the vicinity. Vivienne Duval was listed. So was a
family named Charlet, including a daughter named Jeanine. Jeanine was listed as *"Dienstmädchen, Schloss* Montrond"—maidservant, Château Montrond.

Did this mean Vivienne Duval had been on the deportation
list?

Did it mean that *Obersturmbannführer* Brandt had in some
way amended the list—put her on, taken her off?

Of course, they had not seized *all* the Jews in Vichy. Not all,
by any means. Was it possible that a member of the Charlet family
had in fact committed some offense?

Mrs. Roosevelt pondered for a moment, then made a decision. She left her room and walked next door, to Vivienne's room.
Vivienne had not been sleeping either. She remained fully dressed,
in the clothes she had worn last evening.

"I have brought you something," said Mrs. Roosevelt. "I
found it in *Obersturmbannführer* Brandt's papers."

She handed over the unsigned identity card.

Vivienne Duval clutched the card, pressed it to her breast.
"Thank you!" she whispered. "Thank you!"

"There are some papers as well," said Mrs. Roosevelt. "I
think I understand their significance, and I was thinking of burning
them."

"I would be grateful."

"If you like, come to my room, and we can burn them now."

Vivienne glanced over the sheets of paper, crumpled them,
and put them on the grate in the small fireplace. She laid her old
identity card on top. Mrs. Roosevelt struck a match and lit the fire.

The two women watched pensively as the papers burned.
When the fire was out, Vivienne crumbled the ashes in her hands,
until nothing was left but a fine dust.

"Obersturmbannführer Brandt must have been a good
friend," said Mrs. Roosevelt.

Vivienne nodded.

"I'm glad I found those papers."

"Yes. You are a good friend, too," said Vivienne. Then she smiled wanly and added, "I have been watching for an opportunity to come in here and look for the documents myself."

"I regret to have to tell you, there is a document about your husband, too."

"Saying that he is dead. I know. Brandt told me."

"Were you on the deportation list?"

"No. Not on this one. But if the Nazis do what they are planning to do—that is, deport every Jew in France to Poland—I would have been on the list sooner or later."

"Jeanine Charlet was on the list," said Mrs. Roosevelt. "With her entire family."

"I don't know what criteria they used to select the Jews who were on the list. I believe Brandt knew, but he didn't want to say."

"Would he have acted to save Jeanine yesterday?"

"Yes, and for the same reason that Giesel did: that she knows too much and would probably talk."

"He could not have taken her name off the list, I suppose?"

"He couldn't. The whole town knows that the Charlet family is Jewish. All of them. Not just one grandmother."

"How many know about your grandmother?"

"Not many. The mayor, the priest . . . They won't tell."

"I should imagine, even so," said Mrs. Roosevelt, "that *Obersturmbannführer* Brandt took a grave risk when he substituted papers in your dossier and prepared a new identity card for you."

Vivienne nodded. "He risked his life."

"May I ask why he would do that for you?"

Vivienne stared soberly at Mrs. Roosevelt and did not answer.

"Was there an emotional attachment?" asked the First Lady. "I mean—"

Vivienne sighed. "He said he loved me."

"Did you love him?"

"No. I was grateful to him. I did not love him."

* * *

"There is somethin' wrong with the story," said Kevin when, two hours later, Mrs. Roosevelt told him what Vivienne Duval had said. "Brandt was an officer of the SD. A relationship with a Jewish woman would have ruined him. The high-rankin' Nazi true believers don't even sexually abuse Jewish girls. It would pollute their blood, they say. He'd have been subject to blackmail."

"If he sincerely believed the conspiracy was going to bring down the Nazi hierarchy—"

"He wouldn't add to the danger of that by messin' around with a Jewish woman."

"Then why was he carrying the papers we burned?"

"I don't know."

"Is it likely, do you think," asked Mrs. Roosevelt, "that the papers had something to do with his murder?"

"If any of the faithful Nazis found out he changed a personnel file and issued an altered identity card to protect a Jew, we may be damned sure that has something to do with his murder."

"Right now, I'm deeply concerned with something else," said Mrs. Roosevelt.

"Where is Vicky . . ."

"Yes. Where, indeed."

"Something else," said Kevin. "We've got to get Gertrude Stein and her friend away from here. Things may get . . . sticky at Château Montrond, and we may have to duck out in a hurry."

Kevin met with *Hauptsturmführer* Giesel, making sure that the passes issued by *Obersturmbannführer* Brandt were valid to enable the Misses Stein and Toklas to return home.

Mrs. Roosevelt saw to it that a hearty breakfast, plus a lunch basket were delivered to the two women.

"You have my personal promise that I will do all I can, not just to circulate the word you have brought me, but to inspire an American national commitment to remedying the situation."

"That will not be easy," said Gertrude Stein. "I respect your husband, but I have to doubt that the isolationists and anti-Semites who dominate American politics will allow him to do anything effective to rescue the Jews of Europe."

"I would not be so pessimistic," said Mrs. Roosevelt

"America will not go to war to save the Jews," said Gertrude Stein. "Even if the lives of all the Jews in the world were imminently threatened, America would not go to war to save them. I know there are many in America who care deeply. But the nation as a whole does not care. And that is why Alice and I will stay in France and take our chances. If we die, we will die at the hands of people who think we are a threat. I would rather die at their hands than sit in America and watch Rotarians and Kiwanians ignore the murder of the Jews of Europe."

X

VIKTORIA NEUSTADT—FOR THAT was her name, really—lay in a muddy ditch in a field no more than a hundred meters from Château Montrond, as the sun came up and sheltering darkness gave way to threatening daylight. She tried to focus her eyes on the château, but it was not easy to focus on anything, through blackened eyes swollen almost shut. She coughed and spat blood between cracked and swollen lips. The skin of her shoulders and hips was torn and bloody. The cool, brown mud of the ditch was soothing, and she let herself slip deeper into it.

Like a frog, she lay in the liquid mud, raising her head just enough to afford her a view of the château. If any sort of guard was watching the fields, she had no chance of reaching the walls. If any sort of guard was watching, her chance of slipping past grew worse with every passing minute, as the sun rose higher and flooded the field with light.

Vicky slipped out of the ditch and began to crawl painfully along a furrow, between two rows of some kind of crop, toward the château. She was stark naked. Covered with mud, she was the same color as the field.

If they knew where to look for her, she was dead. But she doubted they did. They had been no clever interrogators, no skilled torturers. They had found her outside after curfew, had decided they did not like her looks or attitude, and had beaten her for no better reason than sadistic pleasure.

Just before they grabbed her, she'd had a moment to toss her pistol away into the darkness. She was alive for that. She was alive, too, because she had been carrying the Baby Browning in a pocket and not in the holster under her clothes, which she could never have gotten rid of in time. She was alive because they had taken her for nothing worse than a curfew violator, carrying no identity card, and so fair game for their bestiality.

Not Germans. French fascists. *Milice.*

They had beaten her. Then four of them had raped her. Then they had beaten her some more.

They hadn't really wanted to know who she was. Not really. Tomorrow would be soon enough to find out. So they had thrown her into the town jail, in the cellar of the Fleurs town hall and left her for the rest of the night.

Only it wasn't a jail. It was just a cellar room, with wrought-iron security bars, half ornamental, bowing out from the sidewalk-level window. She remembered something she had learned during her training—if you were a slight person, not fat, you could slip between any bars you could stick your head through.

She had spent half an hour quietly breaking the glass. Then she had pressed her head between the bars. The effort nearly took her ears off, but she made it. Then she'd had to pull her head back in. Clothes. No. She would have to go through naked. Oil or grease. She didn't have any.

She had stripped and pushed her clothes out onto the sidewalk pavement, to be available when she got through. She had begun the torturous process of forcing her head, then her shoulders, then her body, between the rough, rusty bars. As her skin tore away, she reminded herself repeatedly that this pain was nothing to what remained for her at the hands of the French thugs—or, worse, at the hands of the Gestapo if they decided to turn her over to the Germans.

When she was half out and could not retreat except by the

same slow process that had got her half out, a pair of policemen rounded the corner and marched toward her. She snatched her clothes and pulled them inside the bars. In the awkwardness of her terror, she dropped them. The policemen marched past and failed to notice the head and shoulders of a woman wedged in the bars of a cellar window.

Ten minutes later, leaving much of the skin of her hips and thighs, she was on the street—naked, exhausted, half blind, bleeding, weak.

In the field, halfway between the ditch and the château, she came on a mud puddle and rolled over and over in it, gratefully wallowing in the soothing luxury of the cool mud.

" 'Tis not so bright y've been, y' know," said Kevin. "We're supposed to be a team, y' know—whether you agreed to it or not."

Taking her through little-used passages of the château, Jeanine had managed to bring Vicky unseen to the suite in the tower where Kevin O'Neil was supposed to sleep. Now Jeanine was carrying in buckets of water, since the flow from the tap was so weak. Kevin knelt beside a bathtub and rinsed the mud off Vicky's body

"Y're *hurt*, y' know."

Mrs. Roosevelt entered the bathroom just as the last of the mud was going down the drain and Vicky's injuries were exposed.

The First Lady gasped. "Are we carrying a medical kit?" she asked Kevin.

He shook his head. "Jeanine has gone for Madame Duval."

Staring upward through slits, Vicky tried to speak, was impeded by the painful swelling and cracking of her lips, but persisted and said, "Ice . . . Ice for swelling."

"And a doctor," said Mrs. Roosevelt

Vicky reached up from the tub and grasped Mrs. Roosevelt's wrist. "No! Can't trust . . . Send Jeanine. She knows where to go."

"Who were they?" Kevin demanded.

"*Milice* . . . French Nazis. Two of them former *gendarmes*. Police once. Now . . . Worse than the Gestapo."

"Do you know them by name?" asked Kevin.

"Know one."

"What's his name?"

"Maurice LeFèvre. The leader. They obeyed him."

"Describe him," said Kevin grimly.

"Very handsome," Vicky said. "Smile . . . Thin mustache. French police uniform but German military cap. SS cap. Black."

Mrs. Roosevelt put her hand gently on the shoulder of the injured young woman. "Child . . . Did they abuse you . . . intimately?"

"LeFèvre raped me," said Vicky. "And three others."

"Oh, my dear!"

Vicky snorted. "Twice in Vienna. Now four times here."

"Who in Vienna?" asked Mrs. Roosevelt.

Vicky shrugged. "Nazi street hooligans," she said. "On the street. Right on the street."

Mrs. Roosevelt looked at Kevin and shook her head.

"Need things," Vicky mumbled.

"Yes. What?"

"Ice. Clothes. And a gun."

"Y' wouldn't be thinkin' y're goin' after someone, now would ye?"

"I'm thinking about who might be coming here."

Vivienne Duval entered the bathroom carrying a can of antiseptic powder and bandages and tape. Vicky poured the powder on the bloodiest of her abrasions. It stung, and she winced. Jeanine went for ice. There was not much to be had, only what one old refrigerator froze.

Mrs. Roosevelt handed Vicky a towel. It troubled her that the young woman was sitting in the tub naked, under the eyes of Kevin O'Neil—though the fact did not seem to concern Vicky.

"Are you ready to tell us where you went last night, and why?" Mrs. Roosevelt asked.

"I am your contact with the *Résistance,* as you know. I was on my way to meet with some of them when the *Milice* gang caught me."

"Another murder was committed in the château last night," said Mrs. Roosevelt.

Vicky stared up through the slits of her swollen eyes. *"Who?"*

"We'd like t' know," said Kevin. "A man carryin' a picklock. He'd been workin' on General Rommel's door."

"On General Rommel's door!" exclaimed Mrs. Roosevelt. "I didn't—"

"He was carrying a pistol," Vivienne whispered. "Do you think he came here to—"

"Murder the general," said Kevin. "Seems likely."

"How would he know which room was General Rommel's?" asked Vicky. "He could have come here to kill anyone . . . or maybe just to commit a burglary. If he really came to kill the general, then somebody in this house told him which room is Rommel's."

"Meaning we have a traitor in the house," said Vivienne.

"I wouldn't jump to that conclusion," said Mrs. Roosevelt. "We don't know who the man was or what he was doing."

Vicky stretched out her arms, and all three of the others helped her to climb to her feet. She staggered across the room to Kevin's bed and stretched out on it, being less than careful that the towel covered her.

Jeanine came with the ice. Vicky applied it to her eyes and lips.

"We must go to breakfast with the generals," Mrs. Roosevelt told Vicky. "Bring her coffee, Jeanine. And all the ice you have."

"I've got somethin' else for ye," said Kevin. "In case y' should need the like." He opened a bureau drawer and took out the .22 caliber Beretta that had been carried by the man who now lay under the bed in the room once used by *Obersturmbannführer* Brandt. "Don't scorn it," he said. "Hollow-point bullets. Can take a man's brain apart. Something like 'em did just that to Brother Brandt."

"I regret we have not had time to become better acquainted," said General Rommel to Mrs. Roosevelt over breakfast. He had made a point of sitting beside her. "Do we not make a strange combination: a general of the *Wehrmacht* at a secret meeting with the wife of the President of the United States?"

His English was what he had learned as a schoolboy many years ago: stilted and ungrammatical, but understandable. Her German was about the same. They could converse.

"I fight on the Italianish front in the last war. I am glad it is not on western front. I should not wish to fight Americans. I always them admire."

"I hope our two countries do not have to go to war again," said Mrs. Roosevelt. "So does my husband. That is why I am here."

"I have son," said Rommel. "He is tirteen years old. I wish war to end before he . . ."

"I understand. I have four sons of military age. One is already serving, in the United States Army Air Corps."

Rommel reached inside his gray tunic and withdrew a leather case. He plucked a photograph from the case and handed it to Mrs. Roosevelt. "My son Manfred," he said. "Und my wife Lucie."

The son was a smiling, strong-faced, healthy-looking boy. In the photograph, he stood to his father's right. Rommel, in uniform, showing his *Pour le Mérite* and an Iron Cross at his throat, wearing also the blandest of all possible expressions, stood between his wife and son. The wife wore a mannish suit aı.d hat. Her face, too, was strong; but it was marked with the resigned melancholy of a wife who loves her husband dearly, sees him rarely, and knows she is unlikely to see him more often, not for a long time.

Perhaps Rommel sensed that Mrs. Roosevelt was staring at his wife. "She was dancer," he said. "She has won prizes by dancing."

"She is beautiful," said Mrs. Roosevelt. She meant it. Frau Rommel *was* beautiful, in her own singular way. "And your son is a handsome young man."

"We end the var . . ." said Rommel. His faint, restrained, characteristic smile came to his face. "End the war, I be old general, no work to do, go home and plant garden."

"Maybe you will be Germany's new von Hindenburg," suggested Mrs. Roosevelt.

"Der lieber Gott, nein! Er war sehr dumm."

Mrs. Roosevelt raised her champagne glass. (Champagne at breakfast was outside her experience for the past thirty years, though it had not been unknown in some circles before.) "May we succeed in ending the war, *Herr General*," she said.

Rommel allowed his smile to spread and escape the stern restraint he kept on it. He clinked his glass against hers. "To success, Madame," he said. "I hope we live to see the day when I am privilege to make this good wish at a dinner in White House—and you wish well the new leader of my country at dinner in *Reichskanzlei*."

Hauptsturmführer Giesel saw their toast, smiled, and raised his glass to suggest a second toast. It would be a quiet one, among the three of them, not entrusted to General Rousseau and Gabrielle, or to Sarah Churchill, Kevin, or Vivienne.

"Der Führer," he said; but he said it with such irony that even Mrs. Roosevelt could join in the toast.

"Unserer Führer," Rommel responded, scornfully but not so much so that anyone who heard him would understand the sarcasm.

Mrs. Roosevelt read this exchange as an assurance from General Rommel that *Hauptsturmführer* Giesel was to be trusted.

"I have received no communication from *Obersturmbannführer* Brandt," said Giesel. "I am becoming most alarmed."

"So am I," said Mrs. Roosevelt.

"I wonder if, having seen the conference make a good start, he has not gone on to Berlin."

"That may well be," said Mrs. Roosevelt.

"In that case, he has a problem," said Giesel. "The *Führer* is not there. He is at Rastenberg."

"Where is Rastenberg?"

"It's a dreary little town in East Prussia. The *Führer* has established a headquarters there. That he has gone to a special headquarters in the east is a threatening development. He moved to a headquarters on the western front just before he launched the invasion of France and the Low Countries last year."

Gabrielle, at the orders of General Rousseau, had been to Kevin's suite to see Vicky. She had reported to him, and he moved to speak with Mrs. Roosevelt. He spoke better English than did General Rommel.

"The *Milice*," he said, "are more Nazi than Hitler himself. Anti-Semitic for generations. They think they are fighting Bolsheviks and Jews—which, muchly, they equate. Hoodlums. We must pray they had no idea who she was. More than that, we must pray they did not guess where she went."

Mrs. Roosevelt nodded. "They would be here by now if they guessed."

The generals met again. Sarah Churchill sat with them, as did Kevin. Mrs. Roosevelt went up to talk to Vicky alone.

The young woman lay on Kevin's bed. She had tossed the towel off, because sweat stung. The swelling around her eyes was down a little, and she seemed better able to see. Her lips were more swollen, and her mumbling was more difficult to understand. Mrs. Roosevelt drew up a chair and sat near to her.

"We don't trust each other," the First Lady said. "You have not been fully honest with me. You have your own purposes in coming to Montrond. So, I think, has Kevin. And he hasn't told you what they are, any more than he has told me. I suspect you have not been fully honest with him either. So— I have not told you everything I know, either."

"Understand . . ." Vicky mumbled.

"We will kill ourselves this way," said Mrs. Roosevelt. "We have been here two nights. Each night a murder was committed. The one last night was committed not fifteen feet from where *Obersturmbannführer* Brandt was killed. Last night, *you* were nearly killed. Was it just coincidence that the *Milice* caught you?

Or did someone tell them where to find you?"

"Coincidence."

"Really? Is that all it was?"

Vicky ran her tongue over her broken and swollen lips. "I know one thing," she muttered. "They don't know Brandt is dead. I heard them speaking about him. Brandt this. Brandt that. What would *Obersturmbannführer* Brandt want? What would he expect them to do?"

"Vicky . . . Are you sure they had no idea who you are?"

Vicky shook her head. "I wouldn't be here if they knew. What they did— They wouldn't have done that if they knew."

"Will they guess? Now? Later?"

"They gave me reason enough to be desperate to escape. Probably laughing."

"The two generals are leaving in the morning," said Mrs. Roosevelt. "Kevin and I will be leaving. I—"

"Gertrude Stein and Alice Toklas?"

"They're gone. *Hauptsturmführer* Giesel assured Kevin their passes are good. The question . . . Vicky. You mean to stay here. But you're known. You can go with me."

Vicky shook her head. "Sit in the States and read in the newspapers about what's happening? No. Fight. Maybe get killed. But fight. I fight. I'm, by God, going to—"

Viktoria Neustadt began to sob. Mrs. Roosevelt bent over her and, careful not to touch her more sensitive wounds, embraced her and wept over her.

In the bedroom that had been *Obersturmbannführer* Brandt's, Kevin knelt beside the bed and carefully dragged out the body wrapped in a blanket. He pulled at the head end. Squatting at the other end, General Erwin Rommel pulled at the feet end of the blanket.

With the body lying on the bedroom floor, clear of the bed, Kevin unwrapped the face.

Rommel stared at it for a moment. Then he shook his head.

Kevin rewrapped the face, and the two men shoved the corpse back under the blanket.

In her room in the servants' wing of the château, Jeanine Charlet lay on her bed and wept into her pillow. Outside, a bell rang persistently, even angrily. She was being summoned. Her services as a *Dienstmädchen* were required.

Jeanine got up. She knelt and reached under her bed. From beneath the bed she withdrew what looked like a dust cloth. She unrolled it. From inside the rolled cloth she took out a small automatic pistol. She shoved it into her blouse, where it rested between her breasts, held up and in place by her stout brassiere.

The two generals had reached a detailed agreement on how to end the war. That agreement must now be reduced to a written document, in French and German. Gabrielle, it turned out, was not just a fashion model; she was also a typist. So was *Hauptsturmführer* Giesel. They had brought two typewriters. As the two generals agreed on specific words of text, the two typists created the formal document in two languages.

It was a time-consuming process.

The document began—

PROTOCOL OF AGREEMENT AND UNDERSTANDING

General Paul Rousseau, on behalf of the Provisional Government of France, and General Erwin Rommel, on behalf of the Provisional Government of Germany, do agree and commit themselves and the governments they represent, as follows:

Article the First—

Within five days after the establishment of the Provisional Government of Germany, the Acting Head of State of such Government shall publicly an-

nounce the existence of this Protocol and commit
such Government to the carrying out of its terms.

In that first article the protocol recognized the basic problem. How
was a German provisional government to be established? What
was to be done about Hitler?

Giesel was the only contact the conference had with the state
security apparatus, a tiny element of which had apparently accepted responsibility for the overthrow of the *Führer*. Mrs. Roosevelt wondered if she dared talk to him, to try to discover how much
damage had been done by the murder of *Obersturmbannführer*
Brandt.

As long as he labored at his typewriter, there was no way to
get him aside for a solemn talk.

Before the morning ended, Giesel had to be interrupted.

Jeanine brought the word to Vivienne Duval, who hurried to
the dining room, where the two generals were dictating the protocol to their typists.

"The *Milice!*" she warned. Then she hurried out to the terrace, where Mrs. Roosevelt sat with Sarah Churchill and Kevin.
"*Milice!*"

The men of the *Milice* did not hesitate at the bridge as the
Gestapo and SS contingent had done yesterday. As the generals
and Gabrielle trotted up to their rooms, four uniformed men
marched to the door and knocked hard and loud. Mrs. Roosevelt,
Sarah Churchill, and Kevin rushed from the terrace and into the
house.

Three of the men wore khaki uniforms and looked like German Storm Troopers. Their leader wore dark blue, except for a
black garrison cap.

Vivienne Duval opened the door.

"*Madame Duval?*"

"Oui."

"Bon jour, Madame. Je suis Maurice LeFèvre, Chef du Milice. Je cherche une prisonnière échappée. Une femme."

"Elle n'est pas ici."

Hauptsturmführer Giesel strode into the hall. LeFèvre saluted. Giesel spoke German to the Frenchmen, and LeFèvre conspicuously struggled to understand and to respond in German.

"What are you doing here? Are you not aware that this château is closed to all visitors and intruders?"

"We are searching for an escaped prisoner, *Herr Hauptsturmführer.*"

"Doesn't it occur to you that a château reserved for *Eine Führerschaftkonferenz* is the least likely place in the world where an escaped prisoner might be found?"

"We have reason to believe she came from here and returned here, *Herr Hauptsturmführer.*"

"This conference is highly confidential. The arrangements were made by *Obersturmbannführer* Brandt, on orders from Berlin. Take your hoodlums and get out of here, LeFèvre. If you come here again, I'll have you shot."

LeFèvre flushed. His eyes glittered, and his face turned hot pink. But he shot up his hand in a stiff fascist salute, spun on his heels, and stalked out of the château.

Giesel spoke in French to Vivienne Duval. "I don't know how many more times I can do that," he said.

"He said something absolutely terrifying," Vivienne told the people assembled in Mrs. Roosevelt's bedroom—that is, the First Lady herself and Sarah and Kevin. "He said he had reason to believe his escaped prisoner came from this château and returned here after her escape. How would he know that? How would he know either part of it?"

"Somebody is—" Sarah began.

"Don't jump to that conclusion," said Mrs. Roosevelt. "If someone saw Vicky return here, or even just coming in this direction, they might have deduced that she came from here."

"It is not just a general search of the countryside," said Vivienne. "They climbed onto their truck and went directly back toward the town. They came to search Montrond. So did the Gestapo yesterday."

"How did the generals react to this incursion?" Mrs. Roosevelt asked Vivienne.

"Calmly. I was surprised."

"They have a strong sense of the importance of their work, and they want to finish it before they leave."

"When, incidentally, *are* they leaving?" asked Sarah. "And how?"

"The fewer of us know, the better," said Vivienne.

"My, we do keep secrets, don't we?" Sarah complained. "I am here at as great risk as anyone, and I had supposed I was an ally. Strange alliance, this."

"There is somethin' I believe she's entitled to know," said Kevin, pointing toward the far end of the hall, where a body lay under the bed.

"Yes," said Mrs. Roosevelt. "Yes, you are entitled to know, Miss Churchill, that there was another murder in the château last night. In the hall, just outside General Rommel's room."

"My *God!* Does Rommel know?"

Mrs. Roosevelt shook her head. "And neither does General Rousseau, nor *Hauptsturmführer* Giesel."

"Who? Who was it that was murdered? If—"

"None of us know," said Kevin. "We've looked at the body. None of us recognize him."

"Let *me* see him," said Sarah.

"What? You really need not subject yourself to that ordeal, Miss Churchill."

"You did, I suppose," said Sarah to Mrs. Roosevelt. "And you did," she added, speaking to Vivienne. "You say 'None of us recognize him.' All of you have seen him but me."

"If y' insist," said Kevin.

Vivienne handed him the key to the room, and Kevin led Sarah to the bedroom where Brandt had died, where the unidentified corpse now lay. He unlocked the door, led her in, and locked the door again.

He lifted the low-hanging bedspread that hid the corpse from someone who might casually enter the room. Seizing the blanket that wrapped the body, he slid it across the floor, then unwrapped the face.

"*Lord!*"

"I've seen uglier ones."

"No— I mean, I know him! I know that man! He . . . He's English!"

"Then what th' hell was he doin' here?"

"I don't know. I'm trying to think of his name. I'm . . . trying to think. Cover him up. Let's go back to the other room."

In Mrs. Roosevelt's room, Sarah sat down and shook her head. "That face . . . It's so . . . familiar! He's English. London . . . I used to see him— Where?"

"About your age, I should judge," said Kevin.

"Yes . . . I think I . . . Dancing. Yes, dancing. I remember him dancing. In a club! Yes! Oh, my God! He's Lord William Ramey! Oh . . . I don't have to go back for another look. Bill! Billy! That's who he is!"

Mrs. Roosevelt moved to stand behind the distraught young woman and rest a comforting hand on her shoulder. "Have you any idea why he was here last night?" she asked quietly.

Sarah Churchill sobbed once, then raised her chin and looked up at Mrs. Roosevelt. "I don't know. I have no idea. What do I remember about him? He went to Eton, then up to Oxford. He read . . . What did he read? Oh. Goethe? No. Schiller. He was a student of German literature. Yes. I remember. He spent a summer in Heidelberg. No, not just a summer: a year. He spent a year at Heidelberg. He told funny stories about the Nazis, about their posturing and— He attended a *Parteitag* at Nuremberg. That's how I remember him: laughing at the strutting Nazis parading through the streets of Nuremberg with shovels over their shoulders instead of rifles. He was very funny at cocktail parties, mimicking Goebbels and Hitler! He—"

"He knew Germany well," said Kevin grimly. "That made him a perfect British intelligence officer."

Sarah nodded. "He may have been. So what was he doing here? And who killed him?"

XI

VICKY SLEPT UNTIL NOON. When she arose she was stiff. Her every movement was painful. Standing in the bathroom of Kevin's suite in the tower, she stared at herself in the mirror. Her eyes were black. Her lips were swollen and split.

She returned to the bedroom and picked up the little Beretta that Kevin had left with her. She checked it over. The eight-shot magazine was full. She took it out, pulled the slide twice to be sure the chamber was clear, and pulled the trigger. The *click* told her the action worked. She shoved the magazine in again and worked the slide to put a cartridge in the chamber.

She had formed a determination. She would kill Maurice LeFèvre. Today or tomorrow. This year or next. Sooner or later, she would kill him.

She had someone else to kill. Someone had sent word to Le-Fèvre that she was leaving the château and could be picked up on the way to town. She would kill whoever that one was, too. Le-Fèvre—and someone else—had made a big mistake.

Mrs. Roosevelt had a longtime habit of reducing her thoughts to writing, when she was searching for the solution to a problem. Political problems. Social problems. The problems of the several mysteries she had contributed to solving over the years. She liked to set things out on paper, often on big pieces of paper she could mount on an easel. Here, she could do no such thing. Here, she could only use writing, diagramming, to make notes she could read and then must burn—since she had no confidence her room was not entered and searched when she was downstairs.

She wrote out some questions on a sheet of lined white paper—

(1) How Mme. Duval chance to come on body so soon after murder? Why she prowling house at that hour?

(2) Who Lord William? What doing here? Why someone kill him?

(3) Vicky injured. Not pretending. So—
    a) Where going when left not very long before dawn?
    b) How French fascists know she was coming? Who betrayed her, and how much more has he betrayed, and to whom?

(4) Is it true Kevin has Swiss francs?
    a) If so, why?
    b) If not, why Mme. Duval lie about it?

(5) Why Giesel not more disturbed by absence of Brandt?

When Kevin knocked on her door, she invited him in, and he found her squatting before the fireplace, watching her crumpled paper burn.

"Vicky is awake," he said. "It may be a good idea if we go and talk with her. I mean, you and I alone."

Vicky sat slumped on the bed in Kevin's tower room, still dazed, weakened by pain. She was wearing nothing but a half slip, which she had pulled up under her armpits so it would cover her breasts, even though that brought its hem close to her hips and almost exposed her crotch. Her bloody abrasions were evident.

The .22 Beretta lay within her reach on the bed.

"Let's be very frank, me child," said Kevin. "Did you kill Brandt? You may have had damned good reason to, but did ye?"

Vicky shook her head. "I wish he were alive again, so he could die a second time—not so painlessly. But I didn't do it."

"You knew him before, then?"

"No."

"He was in Vienna when—"

"No, goddammit! I heard his name in Vienna. I never saw him there, never encountered him."

"You are the one who came to me and told me he was dead," said Mrs. Roosevelt. "How did you know?"

Vicky ran the tips of her fingers over the shiny black bruises around her eyes. She drew a deep breath and noisily let it go. "He knew who I am. I don't know if Donovan told him, or if"—she glanced at Kevin—"you did. Or who. I—"

Kevin interrupted. "I didn't tell him. But he knew. He knew who you are, who I am. 'Twas his life he was riskin', and he'd insisted on knowin' exactly who everybody was. His cooperation was so important, it was agreed he should know who everybody is. In point of fact, I meself insisted on knowin' who ye were before I agreed t' work with ye. Th' generals know who we are, you and me. In fact, the only one we don't know who he is, is Giesel. He's a surprise."

"I never heard of him before," said Vicky.

"I b'lieve the lady asked a question. How was it ye came to know Brandt was dead?"

Vicky sighed. "He spoke to me immediately after we arrived," she said. "He called me Jew-girl and told me he expected me to . . . To 'have some fun' with him, was how he put it. He called for me to come to his room Thursday night. I went up. I didn't want what he had in mind. You can't imagine how little I wanted it, how much I would have liked to kill him instead. But we had come here to do something so important that I was willing to make that sacrifice for it."

"Oh, my dear! He, too?"

Vicky glanced angrily at Mrs. Roosevelt. "No. A little . . . play, and then he told me to go down to the kitchen and bring up a bottle of brandy. I went. Jeanine was in the kitchen. The liquor was locked up. I told her what I wanted and why. She said *she* would take the brandy to the room. I supposed she thought I might be taking it for myself. She thought I was your maid, of course, and— Anyway, she insisted she had to take the brandy to the room herself. We went up together. And we found Brandt lying dead. In the five minutes—less—I was gone, someone came in and shot him."

"You didn't tell us this part."

"I knew what you would think. I would not have killed him. He was too important to us. But if he had to be dead, I only wish I could have killed him. He would not have died so easily."

Mrs. Roosevelt studied the young woman's broken face for a moment, then made a decision. "I believe you," she said.

"Thank you," Vicky muttered.

"We've an identification for the man killed in the hall last night," said Mrs. Roosevelt. "Lord William Ramey. British. Have you ever heard of him?"

Vicky shook her head.

"Why did you go out last night?" asked Mrs. Roosevelt. "You were with us very late, and even then went to the town. Why?"

Vicky tried to smile. It was not easy, but a sort of twisted emulation of a smile came to her lips. "Why do you think I was chosen to be with you on this mission?" she asked. "It is because, having escaped from Vienna, I reached Paris, then escaped again, to Vichy. Have you ever heard of a woman called 'Hedgehog'? I pray you haven't. Have you ever heard of an organization the Gestapo calls '*Arche Noah*'—'Noah's Ark'? I pray you haven't."

Vicky shoved a finger between her broken lips and extracted from her mouth a small rubber cylinder to which two tiny silver hooks were attached. She let them look at it for a moment, then reinserted it between her gum and cheek, shoving the hooks between two of her molars and so clamping the capsule in place so she could not accidentally swallow it.

"Cyanide," said Kevin solemnly.

"It's glass inside the rubber," said Vicky. "I'd have to bite down hard on it to break the glass. If I did, I'd be dead in less than a minute—beyond talking, anyway, then dead soon. I am a member of what the Germans call 'Noah's Ark,' what the French call *l'Alliance*. Were you not told this?"

"Not this much," said Mrs. Roosevelt.

"I have heard of this," said Kevin. "The Germans call you Noah's Ark because all your code names are animal and bird names. What is your name, Vicky?"

"*Alouette.*"

"The Lark," said Mrs. Roosevelt. "It seems appropriate enough."

"In the old French folk song," said Vicky, "the feathers were plucked from the lark. My French friends know I was compelled to strip to my underwear and scrub pavements in Vienna. So—"

"Even in such an organization, in such times, there seems t' be a sense o' humor," said Kevin.

"Without which, if we don't die, we might as well," said Vicky.

Mrs. Roosevelt rose from her chair and went to the window, to look out over the comfortable French countryside. She resisted her impulse to go to Vicky and once again gently embrace her. The First Lady knew how to value courage.

"The other question," said Kevin, "was where ye were goin' last night, and why?"

"As I have said, to meet my contact."

"And why did ye need to meet y'r contact so much at this particular time?"

"The Gestapo came here yesterday looking for Jeanine. I mean to find a way for her to escape. You notice she's still here. I thought she might have resources of her own. But she doesn't."

"Goin' out to save this girl, ye might have cost us dear," said

Kevin. "Yerself, for one. Y' damned near did."

"I took my punishment," said Vicky.

"Not the point," said Kevin. "Heroics serve us ill. Y've suffered hell for your venture. Let us hope that's all we suffer for it."

Mrs. Roosevelt frowned and listened to this exchange. She understood what Kevin O'Neil was saying: that the most basic instincts of humanity must be sacrificed in the specific instance to preserve them in the larger sense. That was what war did to men and women. That was why it was such hell. That was what justified the all-but-insane mission she had agreed to undertake, that had brought her to this obscure château in France, where God only knew what calamity might yet follow.

"You were betrayed last night," she said to Vicky. "I cannot believe you were captured by coincidence. We have a traitor here. Who knew you went out? Who knew where you were going?"

"No one," said Vicky. "I spoke to absolutely no one—not about this."

Kevin shrugged and frowned. "Do the telephones work?" he asked.

"They do," said Vicky. "I've heard the kitchen staff call the town."

"Then someone who just *saw* you go, not knowing why, could have phoned the *Milice* headquarters," said Mrs. Roosevelt.

"Someone who was up and watching after two in the morning," said Vicky.

"And it didn't need to be a general alarm. You were on your way into Fleurs. They needed only to watch the road."

"I've got to ask about your interrogation," said Mrs. Roosevelt. "Did they treat you only as if you were a curfew breaker?"

Vicky turned her head aside and stared at the floor. "They were more interested in . . . in what they did to me."

"No interrogation?"

"Not very much."

"Because," said Mrs. Roosevelt, "someone else was going to interrogate you in the morning."

"Someone who had to come from a little distance," said Kevin. "As from Vichy."

"As from Paris," said Mrs. Roosevelt.

"Aye," said Kevin. "They could have interrogated you so severely you would have crunched your capsule."

"They are only beasts," said Vicky. "Animals. Interested chiefly in—"

"Still," Mrs. Roosevelt interrupted, "we must find out who alerted them."

"I would rather finish our business and get out of Montrond, without ever knowing," said Kevin.

A few minutes later, while they were still talking, Vivienne Duval knocked on the door.

"I must warn you," she said. "The château is now under SS guard. About ten men, I think. They came in a truck."

Some of them were visible from the bedroom window: black-uniformed, helmeted SS troopers, armed with submachine guns.

"I've no idea what this means," said Vivienne.

"Have any of them come inside?" asked Mrs. Roosevelt.

"No. They just drove up, jumped down from the truck, and stationed themselves all around the château. I couldn't say the place is surrounded, actually. There aren't that many of them. But no one is going to come or go without their seeing."

Vicky stared down from the window. "We have been betrayed," she said dully. "The whole conference has been betrayed. That's a preliminary contingent. The Gestapo will come next."

"Not necessarily," said Mrs. Roosevelt. "We—"

She was interrupted by a firm rap on the door. *Hauptsturm-führer* Giesel came in without waiting to be asked.

"I came to explain the guard outside," he said. Glancing around the room, his eyes stopped on Vicky, and he frowned. "So. LeFèvre was right. His escaped prisoner *is* here. Well . . . The more reason to have the guard. I ordered them here from Vichy, immediately after LeFèvre and his *Milice* men left. I don't trust LeFèvre not to come back, maybe with one or two Gestapo men with him."

"A confrontation could be very dangerous," said Mrs. Roosevelt.

"There won't be a confrontation," said Giesel. "When word reaches town—and it will—that I've put an SS squad on guard, no one will come near the château."

"Let us hope so," said Kevin.

Giesel turned to Vicky. "How much did you tell?" he demanded sharply.

"Nothing," she answered.

"They beat you, and you said nothing?"

"They didn't beat me for purposes of interrogation," said Vicky. "Just for the fun of it."

"You were a fool to leave here last night," he said. "You risked everything. May I assume you do not intend to leave again tonight?"

"Are you suggesting I need your permission?"

"I suggest you need *someone's* permission to go off on some errand of your own that risks everything we are doing here." He shot a glance at Mrs. Roosevelt. "Someone's permission . . . We can restrain you if we must. After tomorrow, you can go when and where you wish and do what you want. Until then—the guard has orders to shoot anyone who tries to leave Château Montrond or anyone who tries to get in."

"Allow me to change the subject," said Mrs. Roosevelt. "Vicky was not seized by those men last night simply because they were out looking for curfew breakers. Someone had alerted them that she was coming. Someone probably made a telephone call."

"We can find out," said Giesel.

"Can you?"

"Probably. You can't dial calls here. You have to ring an operator at the central switchboard in Fleurs. I would guess that very few calls are made after midnight. The operator on duty last night may well remember if a call was placed between the château and *Milice* headquarters."

"Would you make the inquiry, please?" asked Mrs. Roosevelt.

Giesel turned to Vivienne Duval. "Where is the nearest telephone?"

There was none in the tower, so Vivienne led Giesel and Mrs. Roosevelt to her sitting room.

Giesel took up the ornate French telephone instrument. He flipped the cradle up and down several times to alert the operator. He spoke French—

"This is *Hauptsturmführer* Giesel, adjutant to *Obersturmbannführer* Brandt of the *Sicherheitsdienst*. I am at Château Montrond. I want to know if a call was placed from the château last night. After midnight. Yes. You were on duty? I see. Two calls. One to the LeFèvre residence. Yes. And another? To the Mercier residence. Do you have any idea who placed the calls? I see. A female voice. The same voice, both calls? And— I see. You feel confident of that? I see. How long were the calls? How long was it between the calls? I see. Can you tell us anything more? Very well, Madame. Very well. Thank you."

He smiled faintly as he put down the telephone. "Two calls, the first to LeFèvre, the second to Mercier. The call to LeFèvre was very short. The one to Mercier was longer. The second call was made immediately after the first one was finished. The person who placed the calls was a woman." His smile broadened. "It was not you, Madame Duval. The operator says she knows your voice, and it wasn't you. She says it was not your cook, either. She knows her voice from the calls she makes to the butcher and baker and grocer. So. Someone. A woman."

"Who is Mercier?" asked Mrs. Roosevelt.

"A wine broker," said Vivienne. "He and my father were well acquainted. His house in the largest in Fleurs. Actually, it's outside the town. He cultivates a few vines and presses a little wine of his own."

"Who in the château would have reason to telephone him in the middle of the night?" asked Giesel.

"I can't even guess," said Vivienne.

"How many women are in the château?" he asked.

Vivienne began to gesture in a Gallic way as she named women and counted them off on her fingers. "Myself and Mrs. Roosevelt. Vicky and Gabrielle. The cook. I have four housemaids. One of them is the cook's daughter. The groundskeeper lives in the château, and his wife lives with him. Ten women."

"The operator says you didn't place the calls. She doesn't think the cook did. I can't imagine that Mrs. Roosevelt did."

"We can be confident, I should think, that Vicky didn't do it," said Mrs. Roosevelt.

"That is a logical assumption," said Giesel, "but one that is not necessarily true. It is not impossible that she went voluntarily to *Milice* headquarters, that she had some business with LeFèvre that did not turn out well, and that he and his thugs beat her and threw her out on the street."

"Logically possible," said Mrs. Roosevelt. "But I think very unlikely."

Giesel shrugged. "If I don't return to my typing, the protocol may never be finished."

"Yes, that should have first priority," said Mrs. Roosevelt.

While Mrs. Roosevelt and Vivienne Duval were with Giesel downstairs, Kevin took Vicky to have a look at the body of the man Sarah Churchill identified as Lord William Ramey. "Everybody else has had a look at him. You should, too."

They locked the door from inside and pulled the body once more from under the bed.

"I don't know him," said Vicky immediately. "Never saw the man before."

"You are carrying his pistol," said Kevin.

Instinctively, Vicky touched the leather holster under her left arm, where the .22 caliber Beretta now rested where the Baby Browning had rested before.

Kevin sighed. "Well . . . I suppose we should shove him back under the bed."

"How well did you search him?" asked Vicky.

"Went through his pockets."

She grimaced. "There's nothing I enjoy more than taking the clothes off a corpse. But if you haven't searched him *really thoroughly*—"

The job was not easy. The body was stiff now. Kevin used his knife to cut the clothes. It took a full five minutes to cut and pull the clothes off and leave the body lying naked on the floor.

They cut the clothes apart. The man had carried nothing in his clothes—nothing in the pockets, nothing in the linings—that would have served to identify him.

"It's too perfect," said Vicky. "Pry his mouth open."

Kevin used his knife and forced the stiff jaws to yield. Vicky ran her fingers around inside.

"Here it is," she said. "Just like mine."

She had found a rubber-covered cyanide capsule, attached to the man's teeth with a dentist's silver hooks.

Vicky stared into Kevin's eyes. "You know what we have to do now. Turn him over."

They rolled the body over, face down. Vicky stood up and walked to the window to look out on the sunlit day.

" 'Tis all right, lass," said Kevin. "And ye were right. Nothin' tidy. But here it is, all wiped clean."

She turned and looked down. He was pointing at a small aluminum tube, a little more than three inches long, half an inch in diameter: the sort of thing expensive cigars were packaged in, only smaller. Kevin had removed it from the anus of the corpse.

"Open it," she said.

He nodded. It had a screw-on cap, which he turned and put aside. He put a finger inside the cylinder and drew out a tight roll of currency.

"So. His money. Hidden where only a thorough policeman would find it."

The money was so tightly rolled that it was difficult to straighten it out and examine it.

"*Reichsmarks,*" muttered Kevin. "Not enough to make a man wealthy, but enough to travel around in luxury for quite a time."

Vicky squinted at one of the bills. She still had difficulty focusing her eyes through the swelling. "See how many of them are like this," she said.

Kevin, too, squinted over that particular bill. "Damn!" he said, and he began looking at the others. "Another one. Another. This one's not. This one is. What? All but two."

Vicky nodded, and her lips turned into as much of a smile as they could make. "Tells us something, doesn't it?"

All but two of the *Reichsmark* notes were overprinted with the word AFRIKA. This was army scrip, used to pay the German soldiers of the *Afrika Korps*. It was good money in Europe, and in North Africa it was the only German money the German government would honor. It was the currency used to pay the troops. A deserter or a spy, carrying ordinary *Reichsmarks*, could not spend them anywhere in Africa. Merchants would not accept them, and the banks would not accept them—because the *Reichsbank* would not honor any Germany currency from Africa that did not bear the AFRIKA overprint.

"Maybe he was not who Sarah Churchill thinks he was," said Kevin.

"No, he's exactly who Sarah Churchill thinks he was," said Vicky. "He was working behind the German lines in North Africa. If he needed to use money, that's the kind of money he had to use."

"Then what, do you guess, was he doing here?"

"The Desert Fox," said Vicky. "Are you aware that General Auchinleck, the British commander in North Africa, has sent an order to his officers, directing them to discourage their troops from circulating rumors that Rommel is some sort of supergeneral? Imagine that! They've had to order their troops to accept the idea that he is just another German officer. Can you imagine how much they want to assassinate him?"

"When he is here, negotiating—"

"Kevin! What makes you suppose the left hand knows what

the right hand is doing? What he is doing here is so secret that not five people in the British government know. The rest assume the assassination of Rommel continues to have high priority."

Kevin nodded. "Besides which, this Lord William Ramey was in the field, out of touch."

"He came here to kill him. I think we can be almost certain of it."

"If that is so, then someone had told him which room is Rommel's. He was killed while trying to break into that room."

"Yes, and killed by whom? That's the big question. Do the Germans have a security force in the château, that we don't know about? Is that who betrayed me to the *Milice* last night?"

Kevin shrugged. "General Rommel is a valuable man," he said. "I doubt he is left unprotected."

"But *who?*" Vicky persisted. "Who that we don't know about, may have seen God-knows-what?"

"Who helped Lord William Ramey get in here? That's the question I'd like to see answered."

Vicky sighed. "What's left here?" she asked. "Twenty-four hours? Let the two generals sign that protocol, and then we can all get out of here. I have plans. I have a man to kill."

"LeFèvre?"

"LeFèvre."

"Good luck."

"When you get to the States—"

Kevin interrupted her with a shake of his head. "I'm not goin' to the States. Nor London. Nor Ireland. I'm obliged to get Mrs. Roosevelt back aboard that submarine. Then I'm like you. I've got me own plans."

"I'm glad to see you two," said Mrs. Roosevelt when she met them coming along the corridor, having left the body of Lord William Ramey, now naked but wrapped in a blanket, under the bed. "I've something I want to talk to you about."

"We've come to a couple of conclusions of our own," said

Kevin. "One of which is, maybe we'd ought to put more trust in Sarah Churchill. I'd like to know what she's remembered by now about the man whose body lies in the far room."

"The generals and the *Hauptsturmführer* are hard at work on the protocol," said Mrs. Roosevelt. "Perhaps we should gather on the terrace."

When Kevin appeared on the terrace, ten minutes later, he was carrying an ice bucket chilling a bottle of champagne, also a bottle of Scotch.

Vicky and Sarah expressed a preference for the whiskey. Kevin shook his head, grinned at Mrs. Roosevelt, and poured her a water glass of champagne. "Drink up, ol' girl," he said. " 'Tis good for everything that could possibly ail ye."

Mrs. Roosevelt laughed. She had grown up in households where champagne and other wines, plus liquor, were liberally consumed. Her own reluctance to enjoy these things as much as others did—as much in fact as her husband did—resulted probably from the damage she had seen it do to her beloved father. Then she had lived through Prohibition—though that episode had hardly restrained the people of *her* social class, who had always managed to obtain anything they wanted. She'd sensed over the years that she was protecting Franklin from a tendency to drink just a drop or two more than he should. Now— This bold Irish rogue wanted her to drink a whole bottle of champagne, all to herself. Well, she wouldn't do that, but she raised the big glass, saluted, and took a satisfying swallow of the bubbly white wine.

Kevin unrolled one of the German banknotes he had taken from the tube he'd pulled from the anus of the corpse. He handed it to Sarah Churchill. "Why, d' ye suppose, y'r friend Ramey would have been carryin' a tidy sum in notes of the kind?" he asked.

She frowned over the note for a moment. "He'd been serving in Africa, I should imagine," she said.

"Did he speak German?" asked Vicky.

Sarah snorted. "Of course he spoke German. He was the son of an earl. Twenty-five or thirty years ago, they all spoke it at Windsor Castle. Until bloody recently, you were hard-put to hobnob with royalty if you didn't. Even before the war, even before the last one, my father used to refer to the Hanoverians and their descendants as 'those thick Kraut parvenus.' Yes. Lord William spoke German."

"Do you remember anything else about him, that you didn't remember when we spoke of him before?" asked Mrs. Roosevelt.

Sarah shook her head.

"Is it possible, d' ye think," asked Kevin, "that this man might have had a mission in this war: to kill General Rommel?"

Sarah shrugged. Then she took the question more seriously. "You're saying that— Oh, my God! Oh, my *GOD!* He couldn't have been called off, because people at the level to be entrusted with the plan for this conference would not have known that other types, at a far lower level, were planning— They could never have put such a plan past my father!"

Kevin had begun to nod and continued nodding as the implications impressed themselves on Sara. "There is a sayin' in the espionage business. Operations secrecy has a terrible corollary. Spies have got an awful knack for muckin' up each other's endeavors."

"And getting themselves killed in the process," said Sarah.

"Part of th' game," said Kevin. "Th' unfortunate part is, they do it for sentiment. I venture a bit. But I do it for money."

"How noble."

"How practical."

"I think this is a bit speculative," said Mrs. Roosevelt.

"And worthless speculation if we don't know who killed him," said Vicky.

"When we know what a murdered man was doing just before his death, it becomes easier to understand his murder," said Kevin.

"I . . . want to talk about something a little less speculative," said the First Lady. "Two telephone calls were made from Château Montrond last night after midnight. The first was to Monsieur Le-

Fèvre. The second was to a Monsieur Mercier—or at least to his residence."

"Who is Mercier?" Vicky asked.

"I knew I'd seen the name somewhere recently," said Mrs. Roosevelt. "I had to think about it for a time, trying to remember. Then it came to me. Among the papers in the luggage carried by *Obersturmbannführer* Brandt was a list of the Jews in the town of Fleurs and the neighboring countryside. The Charlet family was on the list. Jeanine was on the list. And so was . . ."

Mrs. Roosevelt paused. She decided not to mention the fact that Vivienne Duval was on the list. "And so was a man named Olivier Mercier. He and his family. They were not selected for the transport to Poland, apparently—as the Charlets were."

"Maybe Jeanine can explain," said Vicky.

VICKY RETURNED TO KEVIN'S room in the tower, to ease her sore body down on a bed and try to recover a little of the sleep she had lost. Vivienne Duval went to the kitchen to give instructions for the final dinner of the conference. Sarah, Kevin, and Mrs. Roosevelt were left on the terrace, the First Lady still with a little champagne left in her glass, with Kevin ready to refill it as soon as he had poured more whisky for himself and Sarah.

"I have a thought," said Mrs. Roosevelt. "That tool Lord William was carrying. I believe you called it a picklock, Kevin. How does it work?"

Kevin shrugged. "You shove the end of it in the lock. Then you pry the tumblers, force them if you have to."

"Will this break the tumblers?"

"Ordinarily not. But it could."

"Scratch them? Leave marks?"

"Probably. And I see what y're drivin' at. Have a bit more champagne, and we'll go see."

"Not *his* door," said Mrs. Roosevelt when they were in the hall upstairs. "I wouldn't want to take the slightest chance of General Rommel discovering us removing the lock from his door. Let's do mine. If my surmise is correct, that will be just as informative."

Kevin carried a big pocketknife. One of the blades was a strong screwdriver. As Mrs. Roosevelt and Sarah Churchill watched, he removed the inside plate from the lock on her door. They saw what she had surmised. The interior of the lock was scarred with deep scratches. They were bright and fresh. The metal had not yet corroded and dulled them.

"So. What does this tell us?" asked Sarah.

"We had wondered," said Mrs. Roosevelt, "how Lord William knew which room was General Rommel's. We had wondered if someone in the château had not been working with him. Those scratches demonstrate that he had used his picklock on this door as well. He'd been going along the hall trying all the doors."

"Then it is not necessarily true," said Sarah, "that he was here to kill General Rommel."

"Maybe he had come to kill *Obersturmbannführer* Brandt," said Kevin.

"I think the fact that he was carrying so much money over-printed AFRIKA pretty clearly tells us he had been in Africa," said Mrs. Roosevelt. "I believe we have speculated correctly about what he was doing here."

"How could he have tracked Rommel from Africa to Château Montrond?" Sarah asked.

"He would not have been workin' alone, in any case," said Kevin. "It is well known that Rommel flies in a distinctive airplane, marked with desert camouflage. Anyone who saw him take off and noticed the course he took would have guessed he wasn't goin' to Berlin. On that trip he'd have had to land and refuel, meanin' in Italy fer sure. When he flew away nor'-nor'west, that meant France. After that, it's a simple matter to radio London, sayin', 'Alert the Free French to watch for th' landin' of a small German airplane marked with Africa camouflage an' advise where the passenger goes.' And—"

"And that message would have gone through British Intelligence without anyone suspecting the subject was Rommel, much less that he was on his way here to try to negotiate a peace."

"Aye, Miss Churchill. It's speculative, as Mrs. Roosevelt is about to tell us, but I b'lieve it's good speculation."

"I'll accept it, as far as it goes," said Mrs. Roosevelt. "The difficulty with it is, it offers us no idea as to who killed the man."

Everyone who had come for the conference assembled on the terrace at six and would sit for dinner at seven-thirty.

General Rommel came down a little early and met Mrs. Roosevelt alone. It was coincidence. They had not planned a private meeting.

"This meeting," he said, "has been as success as I could have hoped. If *Obersturmbannführer* Brandt and his associates can do as they have promise, we may restore the peace."

Mrs. Roosevelt drew a deep breath. "How essential is Brandt?" she asked. "He has been missing two days."

"If he is not being arrested, his absence is not alarm to me. All those SS and SD fellows are big secret-keepers. He may be doing some other service to the plan. I don't think it accident that *Hauptsturmführer* Giesel is here. I think he is ordered to come, because Brandt is away doing something else. All I fear is that the invasion of Russia may come before we can act."

"Even so," she said. "It would be another great error on the part of Herr Hitler, and—"

Rommel shook his head. "Even I will not move against the *Führer* if we are at war against the Asiatic hordes of Bolsheviks. If that happens, he is the only man who can save Europe—even if he is saving it from his own mistake."

"Then all must move quickly," she said.

"We sign the protocol, at dinner."

General Rousseau and Gabrielle arrived, with Vivienne Duval. The French general shook hands again with Rommel.

"If we fail," he said in French, "I wish you survival, *Herr General.*"

Rommel answered in French. "I wish the same for you, *Monsieur le Général.* The years ahead will be hard if we fail. And probably, too, if we don't. But I suggest we meet here again a year after the war. May we hope that the charming Madame Roosevelt will join us then?"

The butler arrived, pushing a cart laden with iced champagne, brandy, and whiskey.

Kevin arrived, then Giesel and Sarah Churchill. Finally, Vicky came to the terrace. Mrs. Roosevelt had insisted on dropping the pretense that she was a maid and identified her as "my bodyguard—I suppose you didn't doubt I had one." She explained Vicky's conspicuous bruises as, "what she suffered fending off the single problem I've had here—and fending it so successfully that none of us need worry in the slightest about what it was."

The explanation did not satisfy the generals at all, but they were satisfied when Giesel smiled and said, "I can endorse the lady's statement. Her . . . bodyguard performed an act of heroism that eliminated the only problem we have had. She was appointed by Colonel Donovan, of whom I am sure you have heard, and even if I had no confidence in her or in Mrs. Roosevelt—which assuredly I do—I would have confidence in Colonel Donovan. Except for the President and Mrs. Roosevelt, Colonel Donovan is the only American who knows we are here, and why."

Tonight for the first time, *Hauptsturmführer* Giesel appeared, not in the jet-black uniform of the SS, but in the field gray of the *Wehrmacht*—with black shoulder and collar tabs bearing the aluminum insignia of the SS. He could not, Mrs. Roosevelt reflected, no matter what he did, look like a soldier, as General Rommel so easily and naturally did. Giesel looked like a fishmonger, looked as though he would have been more comfortable in a long white apron and a boater straw hat, dispensing fish off beds of ice.

The cocktail hour was celebrated with determined conviviality. Kevin kept pushing glasses of champagne at Mrs. Roosevelt, until she became convinced he was trying to amuse himself by getting her drunk. She drank far more than she usually did—or had, for twenty years—but discovered that she still knew the line between amusing herself and drinking too much; and she was able to relax and enjoy the hour as she almost never did a cocktail hour at home.

After all, hazards or no, she had no further responsibilities. She had come here to demonstrate the good faith of the government of the United States in encouraging the two generals and the representatives of the Nazi security forces to meet, and that she had done. She could have wished the protocol the two generals would sign committed their two nations to doing something about the Jews; but she was convinced that the best things that could be done for the Jews was to bring down the Hitler régime and end the war.

She would carry home a copy of the protocol. Gabrielle had typed a second copy of the French version. Giesel promised that a copy of the German version would be ready for her before she left in the morning.

Even if it never went into effect, the protocol would be an historic document.

They sat down to dinner. Before the first course was served, Vivienne Duval rose and tapped a glass with her spoon.

"Before we enjoy dinner," she said, "we are to witness an event that may change the history of the world. General Rommel and General Rousseau will now sign the protocol: the agreement they have reached during these two and a half days of negotiation."

The generals did sign. Each made a brief statement first; then each signed.

Mrs. Roosevelt reflected once again that if this protocol went into effect to achieve peace for Europe, it would have been a peace arranged by two generals with little appreciation of the aspirations of peoples, two generals who had, in effect, drawn pencil lines across Europe and proclaimed them borders. How many times had it been done before? And how many times had the peace lasted?

Then there were toasts. The solemnity was shallow and artificial, she judged. Yet . . . if by some remote chance this thing worked, what this strange clandestine conference would have achieved would stand as a watershed conference as important as any European monarchs and statesmen had ever attended.

Mrs. Roosevelt was seated beside General Rousseau.

"I trust the German," he said quietly to her. "In fact, I trust both these Germans. Do you have any idea where *Obersturm-bannführer* Brandt is?"

Mrs. Roosevelt decided to tell him. "Brandt is dead," she whispered. "Murdered, here in the château the first night. *Haupt-sturmführer* Giesel does not know."

"Then all is lost," said General Rousseau sepulchrally.

Mrs. Roosevelt shook her head. "There are others committed to the plan. General Rommel so assured me. Giesel has said as much."

"If our plan fails," said the florid French general, "we must deny we ever saw each other."

"Of course," she said. "And everyone at this table has a personal as well as a patriotic motive for keeping the secret."

General Rousseau bowed to the First Lady. "Allow me to express my profound gratitude to you," he said. "We will not see each other again soon. Immediately after dinner, I am leaving for Paris. General Rommel is leaving for North Africa. By your presence here, you have proved that your husband and his government takes seriously the possibility we have achieved something good these two days. By her presence, Mademoiselle Churchill has proved the *bona fides* of her father. You have made no commitment. But we read a commitment in your presence. *Vive les Etats Unis! Vive la France!*"

After a final round of toasts, the two generals and Gabrielle left the château in cars that were waiting for them and sped away into the night.

Hauptsturmführer Giesel had suggested, just before the generals left, that the rest of the party should reassemble at the dinner table ten minutes later. His manner made it clear this was not just a suggestion but a summons.

So they sat down around the table again. The dishes had been cleared by the staff. Glasses, wine, and liquors remained.

It was not difficult to read the people. Vivienne Duval was plainly worried as to why they were here. She sat stiffly, smoking a cigarette, which Mrs. Roosevelt had not before seen her do. Vicky was sullen and defiant. Sarah Churchill was silent, yet apparently confident. Kevin bore an appearance of calm.

Kevin poured whiskey for himself. Sarah snatched the brandy bottle from the middle of the table and poured herself a generous splash. Vicky reached for the bottle then and poured her snifter half full.

"Now that the generals have gone," said *Hauptsturmführer* Giesel, "I think it is time for someone to tell me what has happened to *Obersturmbannführer* Brandt."

He spoke English, and their conversation proceeded in English.

"He's dead," said Kevin bluntly, without hesitation.

"Yes, I had guessed that," said Giesel. "Does anyone wish to tell me how it happens to be so?"

"We wish we knew," said Mrs. Roosevelt. "He died in his bedroom Thursday night. Someone shot him."

"Someone disposed of the body, of course," said Giesel.

"Someone did, indeed," said Kevin. "A great deal was at risk here. We hardly dared call the police."

"And hardly dared confide in me," said Giesel indignantly.

"Well, now, tell me, me lad," said Kevin. "Should we have trusted you so fast, considerin' that we didn't know you?"

Giesel stiffened. "*Obersturmbannführer* Brandt committed treason. So have I. If my presence at this meeting becomes known, I am a dead man."

"Assumin' what we came here to do doesn't happen."

"Assuming that," said Giesel. "But we are involved, most of us, in survival. We damage our chances by keeping secrets from each other. So . . . To begin with, where is the body of *Obersturmbannführer* Brandt?"

"Down th' well," said Kevin.

"Am I to assume you have no idea who killed him?"

"That is not *exactly* true," said Mrs. Roosevelt. "We have some clues."

"And so do I," said Giesel ominously.

"We may be threatened by something more immediate," said Mrs. Roosevelt. "Someone in the château betrayed Vicky to this man LeFèvre. So far as I can tell, we may have suffered no other betrayal of confidence. But I think we had better somehow deal with that one."

"Aye, *Herr Hauptsturmführer*," said Kevin. "If I may be so bold, I think ye might well order Monsieur LeFèvre to attend on us—and you and I can flip a coin as to which one blows his head off."

"A tempting proposition," said Giesel. "But simplistic. Having eliminated LeFèvre, we are still left with his informant unidentified."

"I agree," said Mrs. Roosevelt. "The key to identifying his informant lies in the two telephone calls made from here last night. One to LeFèvre, one to the Mercier residence."

"I know the Merciers," said Vivienne. "It is difficult to imagine why—"

"I suspect," said Mrs. Roosevelt, "that diverse elements of our mystery come together in that telephone call. I've given it a great deal of thought."

"Productive thought, I hope," said Vivienne Duval acerbically.

"*Hauptsturmführer* Giesel—"

"Please, dear lady. My name is Konrad. Our lives and fates are far too much entangled for us to stand on formalities."

She nodded. "Konrad. That *is* easier, is it not? So, Konrad— Are you aware of the . . . adjustments *Obersturmbannführer* Brandt made to certain files in the Vichy offices of the *Sicherheitsdienst?*"

Giesel nodded. "I know what you mean. I was his adjutant."

"Yes. Now. Last week some twelve thousand Jewish people were arrested and marked for transportation to Poland, to what fate only God knows. Tell me, Konrad, was Madame Duval on that list?"

"No," said Giesel. "She was never on the list."

"There is a file—a very large file, I should suppose—containing the names of Jews living in Vichy. The victims of the transportation order were taken from that list, I should imagine."

"Exactly so," said Giesel.

"A very small element of that file—no more than a single page—listed the known Jews in Fleurs and vicinity."

"Yes. Exactly so."

"And Madame Duval's name was taken off that list by *Obersturmbannführer* Brandt, so she was not susceptible to arrest and deportation to Poland."

Giesel nodded.

"How the hell could he get away with that?" asked Vicky.

Giesel smiled thinly. "He did it a long time ago. Then he saw to it that the clerks responsible for those files, French or German, were transferred to other work, so there was no possibility of their noticing the change."

"Which was all very well for the central office in Vichy," said Mrs. Roosevelt, "but some local people—let us say Maurice Le-Fèvre knew who was on the original list."

"LeFèvre is a French fascist," said Giesel. "More Nazi than Hitler. An anti-Semite of many years' standing. Yes, he knew the list."

"And knew how to use it to his advantage," said Mrs. Roosevelt. "Yet, being a subordinate, a minor subordinate, of *Obersturmbannführer* Brandt, he would never have dared suggest the list failed to name a particular Jew in which he knew Brandt was interested: that is, Madame Duval."

"What are you trying to say?" Vivienne Duval demanded angrily.

"That Brandt took you off the list of Jews," said Kevin. "And for good reason, I dare say."

"Not the major point for the moment," said Mrs. Roosevelt. "LeFèvre had access to the list. The Charlet family was on it. They were never taken off. The family was arrested, except for Jeanine, who was working here and not to be found in the family home. So—"

"What do you suspect?" asked Giesel.

"Well . . . Let us place a telephone call," Mrs. Roosevelt suggested.

As before, Vivienne Duval led Mrs. Roosevelt and *Hauptsturmführer* Giesel to her study. Giesel placed the call to the Mercier residence but at the First Lady's suggestion handed her the instrument as soon as the telephone began to ring.

"*Allo.*"

"*Qui est à l'appareil?*" Who is speaking?

"*Je suis Madame Mercier. A qui voulez-vous parler?*"

"*Je voudrais parler à Madame Charlet, s'il vous plaît.*"

"*Elle s'est couchée.*" She has gone to bed.

"*Ah, so. Merci, Madame.*"

Mrs. Roosevelt put down the telephone. She turned to the others and shook her head. "Madame Charlet, who we would suppose had reached Poland by now, is in bed in the Mercier house. And that, I am afraid, tells us who our traitor is."

"LeFèvre!" said Giesel. "He took the Charlets off the transport, so he'd have someone in this house who could tell him what has been happening here."

"Which makes Jeanine our spy and traitor," said Vivienne.

"Yes. Where is she?"

"In her room, or in the kitchen, I should think."

Giesel nodded curtly and stalked off to seize Jeanine Charlet.

"I am afraid it is not going to go well with her," said Mrs. Roosevelt quietly to Vivienne.

* * *

They returned to the dining room, where shortly Giesel reappeared, dragging the terrified Jeanine by the arm. She was wearing the gray dress and white apron and cap of a housemaid. He pushed her down in a chair. Vivienne poured a generous amount of brandy and pushed the glass across the table to her.

"She admits it," said Giesel in French. The conversation that followed would be in French, the only language in which Jeanine was fluent.

Jeanine glanced around the table, her eyes hard with fear yet also with resentment as Mrs. Roosevelt judged.

"It saved my family's life," said Jeanine. "And mine. Maybe only temporarily. Temporarily may prove long enough, who knows?"

"Tell us exactly what you did," said Vicky.

"*He* did it. Maurice LeFèvre. He sent a man to arrest me. Thursday afternoon. I supposed that was what it was: that I was being arrested. I was on the list for the transport and hadn't been picked up only because I was here at the château, not at home. The man took me to town—but not to the town hall, to LeFèvre's house. He told me there was a secret meeting going on at the château. He said *Obersturmbannführer* Brandt had arranged for six cases of fine champagne to be delivered, plus supplies of food like we haven't seen in France in a year. He made me a proposition. If I would inform him of who came to the château and what they were doing, he would rescue my family from the transport. It was still being assembled. My family was still in the town jail. They wouldn't be moved to the trains for another day or so."

"What could she do but agree?" asked Mrs. Roosevelt.

"So what did you do?" asked Vivienne.

"I looked around. I looked at the guests. I knew who General Rousseau was. The German general . . . I didn't know. I listened until I heard someone mention his name. I recognized Mrs. Roosevelt immediately. During dinner I left the château and went into town, crossing the fields to be as quick about it as possible—and to avoid the police."

She paused and at one gulp drank half the brandy Vivienne had poured for her.

"I went to LeFèvre's house, as he had told me to do. I told him what I'd seen and heard. When I told him I'd seen Mrs. Roosevelt here, he laughed at me and said that was impossible. The tall woman had to be Frau Rommel, he said. Or someone else. He wanted to know if *Obersturmbannführer* Brandt was at the château. I said there was an SS officer but that I wouldn't recognize *Obersturmbannführer* Brandt; I had never seen him. That was my next task, he said: to identify the SS officer for sure. He told me to look at the black collar patches. The insignia of an *Obersturmbannführer* was four aluminum squares above two stripes."

She paused and looked at Vicky.

"That's why I insisted on carrying the brandy up. I had to get a close look at the SS officer, to read his insignia. I was to telephone LeFèvre as soon as I found out. He said it was extremely important to him to know if *Obersturmbannführer* Brandt was at the château."

"Then you came back here?" said Vivienne.

"Well . . . He took me in his bedroom and made me do some things I didn't want to do, don't want to talk about. He said he could save me and my family permanently if I was good to him."

"You had a busy night," said Vicky dryly. "You went into Fleurs, reported to LeFèvre, were subjected to his 'favors,' then came back out here and were in the kitchen at the right time to—"

"I didn't murder *Obersturmbannführer* Brandt," said Jeanine. "And I don't know who did."

"No, I'm damned well sure you didn't," said Vicky. "And probably don't know who did. But tell me something— We took the *Obersturmbannführer's* car to town and left it in a garage. Whose garage?"

Jeanine turned to Giesel. "Monsieur Mercier's."

"You went to see if your family was in fact at the Mercier house," said Giesel.

"Yes. I saw they were there. Safe for the moment."

"And you telephoned them last night to make sure again," said Mrs. Roosevelt. "That was the call you made just after you had called LeFèvre to tell him Vicky was coming into town."

"From the description I gave of your maid," said Jeanine to Mrs. Roosevelt, "LeFèvre guessed who she is. Of the *Maquis*. Wanted by the Gestapo. He was most grateful to know she was coming."

"Oh, thank you," Vicky sneered.

Jeanine stared at Vicky. "Would you have done differently, if your family's life was at stake?"

"Did you tell Monsieur LeFèvre that *Obersturmbannführer* Brandt is dead?" asked Mrs. Roosevelt.

Jeanine shook her head. "No," she said. "If he'd known that— Well . . . It was only his subordination to the *Obersturmbannführer*, his fear of him, that prevented his descending on the château with a squad of armed *Miliciens*."

"And just what did he intend to do with me?" asked Vicky.

"Hold you until he found out exactly what was going on at Château Montrond. Then, probably, turn you over to the Gestapo, for the credit that would have won for him. Or maybe—maybe you would have become a trading marker he could have somehow used."

"Which of us gets the privilege of blowing his head off, *Herr Hauptsturmführer?*" asked Kevin.

"The one who exposes the murderer of *Herr Obersturmbannführer* Brandt," said Giesel.

"I am afraid it is rather obvious who did that," said Mrs. Roosevelt.

"Indeed?" said Giesel.

"Ye think ye know, do ye now?" asked Kevin.

"I'm reasonably confident I do," said the First Lady. "The person I have suspected all along, who killed him for as good reasons, almost, as Jeanine had for betraying us all."

"I believe you had better state your case," said Giesel.

"Before I do," Mrs. Roosevelt said to him, "please tell us what you know about the relationship between *Obersturmbannführer* Brandt and Madame Duval."

"I was his adjutant. I knew he was enamored of her. He did his own investigation and learned that her husband was dead."

"*Was* he dead?" asked Vivienne bitterly. "Or did Brandt arrange his death?"

"I promise you, Madame, on a word of honor you may not wish to take, that of an officer of the SS, that your husband died of wounds received in battle in May, 1940. *Obersturmbannführer* Brandt learned of his death, upon inquiry. He had nothing to do with causing it."

" 'Enamored of her,' ye say?"

"And of Château Montrond," said Giesel. "He could see no reason why he should not live here as master of the château, husband of the heiress."

"The château belongs to my father," said Vivienne.

"Who fled France in 1940, leaving you here."

"That was my choice."

"Those who fled may find it difficult to recover their property—under prewar French law, not to mention difficulties they may experience from the new French government. In any event, the *Obersturmbannführer* hoped to retire to Montrond and live here with a charming Frenchwoman."

"He made that plain," said Vivienne coldly.

"Yes, and he went to a great deal of trouble to make it possible: to have your name stricken from the Jew-list, to name one difficulty."

"Yes, he did. And he did a great deal more for me—including the arrangements to bring this important meeting to Château Montrond. So, if I am about to hear a suggestion that *I* killed *Obersturmbannführer* Brandt or consented to his death, I should like to know what would motivate me to kill a man who was my benefactor."

"Perhaps we should review the evidence that suggests you killed him," said Mrs. Roosevelt.

"Let us do that, by all means."

"First, let me tell you what I think happened," said Mrs. Roosevelt. "You had determined to kill *Obersturmbannführer* Brandt—for motives you can give us, if you wish. You came to his room in the middle of the night, expecting he was asleep. You used your key to open his door, and to your surprise you found him awake and dressed. You had no way to know that Vicky had been in his room and had left only a minute or so before to go to the kitchen for a bottle of brandy. You closed the door and engaged in some kind of conversation with the *Obersturmbannführer*. In the course of the conversation, you saw your opportunity and shot him to death. You used a small-caliber pistol that made only a little noise."

"Speculation . . . pure, wild speculation."

"You opened the door a little to check to see if the report of the little pistol had disturbed anyone. You heard Vicky and Jeanine coming up the stairs. You may even have seen them. So you closed the door and retreated into the room. By the time the two young women entered, you had thrown yourself on the floor and rolled under the bed. They discovered the body. Jeanine was terrified. Vicky told her to return to the kitchen and wait. Vicky said she would go for help—by which she meant, though she may not have said so, that she was coming to me and to Kevin O'Neil. As soon as they were gone, you emerged from under the bed and left."

"Prove it," said Vivienne Duval.

"*You've* proved it," said Mrs. Roosevelt.

"How?" Vivienne sneered.

"A few hours after the murder," said Mrs. Roosevelt, "you asked Vicky where you might find the body of *Obersturmbann-führer* Brandt. Presumably, the only people who knew he was dead were Vicky and Jeanine, who found his body, I myself, and Kevin O'Neil who dropped the body down the well—which he did, incidentally, *Hauptsturmführer* Giesel, in the hope we could save the conference and not have it abruptly terminated by word of the murder of the *Obersturmbannführer*. Unless Jeanine had told you of the murder—"

"*I didn't,*" muttered Jeanine.

Mrs. Roosevelt smiled at Jeanine, then spoke again to Vivienne Duval. "You said you knew he was dead. You said you knew he had been shot in the back of the head. How could you have known that?"

"I was wakened by the sound of the shot," said Vivienne.

"That is odd," said Mrs. Roosevelt. "General Rommel's room was directly across the hall. *He* was not wakened by the shot. General Rousseau and Gabrielle were in the adjoining room. *They* were not wakened. But you, two doors down the hall, were."

"I sleep lightly. I know the sounds in my own house."

"Let us suppose that you were wakened by the sound of the shot. Let us suppose you were not even asleep and heard the shot. How did you know the sound came from the room occupied by *Obersturmbannführer* Brandt? How could you tell the shot was fired in that one room and not in any of the others?"

"I had a sense that—"

"So you took your master key, walked down the hall, opened the door and saw the body of *Obersturmbannführer* Brandt, killed by a bullet to the head."

"Yes, exactly."

"Then where were you when Vicky and Jeanine came back with the brandy? Vicky says she was gone less than five minutes. Jeanine can confirm it. In a period of four minutes at most, more likely three or two, you heard a shot, came to discover a murdered man lying on the floor of his bedroom, and disappeared."

"I went to get help," said Vivienne Duval. "Time it. You'll see it's the truth. I had plenty of time to—"

"The next morning," Mrs. Roosevelt interrupted, "you pointed an accusing finger at Vicky and asked her where she'd hidden the body."

"I knew she was a member of the *Maquis.*"

"You say you went to get help. How long was it before you returned to *Obersturmbannführer* Brandt's room?"

"I'm not sure."

"Your best guess."

Vivienne Duval shrugged. "Ten minutes. Twenty minutes."

"Really? So short a time? You came back to the room to find the body gone. Not only that, but some of the man's luggage was gone. And I can tell you, Madame, that I had spent some considerable time with that luggage, scanning the papers and photographs it contained. Not only that, but after Kevin disposed of the body, he came to my room and we discussed the contents of the luggage for some time. And only then did I hear you and your servants in the hall, going to the room from which the body had been removed."

"I had to wake two men."

"Did it take an hour and a half? And why did you bring two men to the room?"

"I, too, saw the necessity of hiding the body."

"You lied to *Hauptsturmführer* Giesel," said Mrs. Roosevelt. "You told him you were wakened by the headlights of *Obersturmbannführer* Brandt's car. I can understand your lying. None of us as yet had any confidence in Konrad Giesel. You could have simply said you didn't know where the *Obersturmbannführer* had gone, or when. Instead, you invented a lie. From that moment on, I suspected you."

Vivienne Duval looked at Giesel. "Suppose I did kill him. What happens?"

Giesel glanced around the table, his eyes stopping for an instant on each face. "We have to trust each other," he said. "Not one of us survives if we don't. Not one of us. Not even you, Mrs. Roosevelt."

"Why did you kill him, for Christ's sake?" Vicky demanded of Vivienne. "In the middle of a conference that—"

Vivienne raised her chin high, stretching the tendons in her neck. "My husband was alive as recently as February," she said. "A released prisoner sent the word. He had seen Emile in hospital,

then in a prison for French officers. The letter Brandt showed me
was a forgery. He was a capable forger. Emile may yet be alive, if
der Obersturmbannführer did not arrange his death."

"But—"

"If I had married Brandt, as he was demanding I do, I am sure
he would have arranged the death of Emile—if he hadn't already.
He wanted to live here. This was to be his retirement. If the conference succeeded, he would have demanded Montrond as his reward
from a grateful French government. And I— I would have had to
live with a *beast!* He was no normal man. It was no wonder he had
never been married. No decent woman would have tolerated the
indecencies he demanded! Of course, I . . . My option was the transport to Poland. I faced years, maybe the rest of a lifetime, accom-
modating myself to his filthy demands. You didn't understand all
this, *Herr Hauptsturmführer?*"

Giesel shook his head with nervous rigidity.

"You lie. He demanded indecencies of you, too. You're glad
he's dead. That's why you came here and assumed his position in
the conference. You protested his absence, pro forma; but you really didn't care. If you didn't know he was dead, you hoped he
was."

"I also want to protect the purpose of this conference," said
Giesel. "Brandt would have done what he promised: murdered the
Führer if he could find the chance. But there are others. I don't
give a damn who killed Brandt. I am far more worried about Le-
Fèvre."

MRS. ROOSEVELT WAS WAKENED by a thunderous banging on her door. She snatched up a robe, and opened the door to find both Kevin and Vicky.

"I've transmitted the 2391? code," said Vicky ominously.

"But why? What's wrong?"

"At dawn, the Germany army invaded Russia," said Vicky. "Maybe a hundred divisions. It's Blitzkrieg, like France in 1940. An hour ago, Goebbels broadcast the declaration of war. Everything we came here for is—" She turned down the corners of her mouth and turned up the palms of her hands. *"Kaputt."*

"Of more immediate interest t' us . . ." said Kevin. *Hauptsturmführer* Giesel has decamped, with the squad he had around the château. He can't afford now to admit he ever saw us, I imagine."

"What do we do?" asked Mrs. Roosevelt.

"The code will bring immediate assistance," said Vicky. "From the *Maquis*. From *l'Alliance*. But immediate may be an hour or so. We must destroy everything. Papers. Copy of the protocol, which is meaningless now, anyway. We grab some food and get out of here. There's a rendezvous point down the river. It wouldn't be good for long, but it will be good for long enough.

That, incidentally, is where I was going when I encountered Monsieur LeFèvre: to meet the people who will be working with us and settle the final details of the escape from Montrond."

"What about Miss Churchill?" asked Mrs. Roosevelt.

"She will have to go with us. Her people were coming separately, later. Later will not be soon enough. We've got to get out of here now!"

"Who threatens?" asked Mrs. Roosevelt.

"Les Miliciens," said Vicky. "Maurice LeFèvre. Remember what Giesel told you about him: more Nazi than Hitler himself."

"More Catholic than th' Pope," said Kevin.

"I will dress," said Mrs. Roosevelt.

"I'll stay with you," said Vicky. "And start burning things. Everything but your passport, please. Especially Brandt's documents."

"Oh . . . What of Vivienne and Jeanine?" asked the First Lady.

"That's up to them," said Vicky. "They can go into the hills with the *Maquis,* or take their chances some other way."

"I'll be rousin' them," said Kevin.

Fifteen minutes later they were ready to abandon Château Montrond—Mrs. Roosevelt, Vicky and Kevin, Sarah Churchill, Vivienne Duval, and Jeanine Charlet.

The route was out a back gate and into the fields where a summer crop of mustard was high enough to shield them if need be. In fact, as they neared the river, they would simply lie in the mustard and watch for the arrival of the men and women of the *Maquis*: the armed element of the *Résistance* that was active here in rural France, where from time to time it actually controlled a range of hills or a valley.

Vivienne and Jeanine had not hesitated in deciding they would leave the château. Jeanine had taken a moment to telephone the Mercier home and warn her parents. When they joined the others to leave, these two women were both carrying small pistols. No one needed to be told that the little automatic carried by Vivienne Duval was the gun she had used to kill *Obersturmbann-führer* Brandt.

Kevin was carrying a small black leather valise. Vivienne caught the eye of Mrs. Roosevelt and nodded at the black bag.

They gathered at the rear of the château, near the well where the body of the *Obersturmbannführer* lay weighted down under the dirty water.

Kevin unlatched the solid wooden gate and swung it outward.

"Thank you. I was wondering just how I was going to open the gate. And— I see everyone's assembled. That means we won't have to search them out."

Maurice LeFèvre stood grinning at them, a Schmeisser submachine gun levelled at Kevin. Four other *Miliciens* held submachine guns on the five women.

Speaking French, LeFèvre ordered the group to toss their pistols on the ground. Then, as his men threatened with their submachine guns, he searched each one of them to be sure no one had a hidden weapon. Kevin did—his knife. Then LeFèvre ordered them to step back several paces from the weapons that lay on the ground.

He walked closer to the group and spoke to Mrs. Roosevelt. "Jeanine thinks you are the wife of the President of the United States," he said with a grin. "I can see the resemblance. Of course . . . I was just as wrong. I guessed you were Frau Rommel. I imagine we'll find out who you are, soon enough."

Kevin spoke. "LeFèvre." He tipped his head to suggest they move a few steps apart. "I have a proposition I think will interest you."

LeFèvre shrugged and walked a few steps away from the group and his men. Kevin joined him.

"How would you like fifty thousand Swiss francs? In gold."

"A ransom?"

"Why not?"

"Where is this money?"

"Let's go inside and talk about it," said Kevin. "No need for everyone out here to know. I assume you don't want to share the money with . . . them."

"All right. Inside."

"I'll need my valise."

"I am sure it has a gun in it," said LeFèvre. "Not a very clever ploy."

"*You* pick it up. *You* carry it."

LeFèvre put his Schmeisser aside, leaning it against a wall. He drew a Luger from its holster and ostentatiously flipped off the safety. He held the pistol in his right hand and reached down with his left to pick up the valise. He grunted with surprise, finding the valise heavier than he could have imagined.

He nodded at Kevin. Kevin marched back into the main building of the château. LeFèvre came behind him, holding the Luger pointed at his back.

Kevin led LeFèvre into the small dining room, where the portrait of the bare-breasted Françoise stared down from the wall with an impudent smile.

"Why don't you put the bag on the table and open it?" Kevin asked.

LeFèvre nodded. He hefted the bag onto the table, where it struck the smooth, polished surface with a loud thump. He held the Luger pointed at Kevin's belly while he opened the catch and then opened the bag.

He glanced into the depth of the valise. It was three-quarters filled with loose gold coin, worth fifty thousand francs at the very least, and probably more, the shiny gold glinting in the bright light from the windows that faced the Loire.

LeFèvre was startled. His mouth fell open, and he stared at the hoard of gold.

Kevin had known the man would be mesmerized, at least for an instant. He had counted on that. In that instant of LeFèvre's inattention to him, Kevin struck. He grabbed the barrel of the pistol and shoved it into LeFèvre's belly, so LeFèvre would not dare pull the trigger. As LeFèvre began to struggle, shoving the pistol back around, Kevin's knee shot into his crotch, crushing his male parts. Overcome by excruciating pain, LeFèvre weakened so much that he began to drop to his knees. Kevin wrenched the Luger from LeFèvre's hand; and, still clutching it by the barrel, raised it and brought the butt down on LeFèvre's skull with all the force he could muster.

Returning the safety lever to the On position so as to avoid accidentally firing the pistol, Kevin used the Luger as a bludgeon and grimly beat LeFèvre to death.

Carrying the black bag, he trotted through the halls and to the tower where he'd slept the past three nights. The Schmeisser submachine gun was still under the bed. He pulled it out and ran through the corridors again.

Kevin reached a window where he could see the rear courtyard. The five women still stood in a little knot, conspicuously apprehensive. The four *Miliciens* stood ten feet from them, cradling their submachine guns on their arms. Three of the four men had lit cigarettes. They were at ease, keeping a close watch on the women but not holding the muzzles of their guns on them.

Kevin raised the Schmeisser to his shoulder. This model of submachine gun had two triggers, one behind the other. If the shooter pulled the front trigger with moderate pressure, the gun fired in semi-automatic mode—loosing one shot with each pull. If the shooter pulled harder, the front trigger would shove the rear trigger back, causing the Schmeisser to go into full-automatic mode, firing a stream of bullets as long as any remained in the magazine.

The magazine was full. He had thirty-two shots.

Kevin raised the Schmeisser to his shoulder and took aim on one of the *Miliciens*, on the one who seemed most alert. The barrel of the submachine gun was not long, and it had no great reputation for accuracy. Kevin aimed carefully and squeezed off a shot through the glass which erupted into flying shards under the impact of the 9 mm bullet.

The *Milicien* dropped his gun, clutched his chest with both hands, and toppled forward.

With the others raising their weapons, possibly to shoot at the five women, Kevin had no more time for careful aim. He pulled hard on the triggers, and the Schmeisser bucked and roared and shot a stream of steel-jacketed bullets at the other three *Miliciens*. They jerked and staggered under the impact of this deadly fire.

Kevin ran through a hall and down stairs. He ran out into the open just in time to see Vicky put the muzzle of her pistol to the head of the first *Milicien* he had shot and put a bullet through the man's head. As he walked toward her, she did the same to another man.

Kevin went to the well and dropped the Schmeisser into the water. He did not want anyone to find out whose fingerprints were on it. Not his own. Not the person who had put it under his bed.

He clutched the handle of the black leather valise in his left hand.

They crawled through the mustard field, under a bright morning haze that diffused the sunlight and blurred the shadows. The sound of firing at Château Montrond had certainly been heard. Kevin carried the Schmeisser that had been LeFèvre's. Even Mrs. Roosevelt had moved her holster outside her khaki clothes, to put her pistol within easy reach.

It was Sunday morning. They could hear the church bells ringing in Fleurs. It was difficult on Sunday morning, probably, to roust out troops to search the fields. This was Vichy France, under the tyranny of the SS and Gestapo but not occupied by the *Wehrmacht*. Even the *Miliciens*, who were bound to be infuriated when the bodies of Maurice LeFèvre and his men were found, were at home or in church. The escaping party heard trucks on the road, but there were—maybe—not enough men available to search the mustard fields and the woods along the Loire.

Given time . . .

But the Vichy authorities were not given time. The 2391? code had been sent, and emergency help was moving.

The first *Maquis* arrived before the sun was high.

Vivienne and Jeanine did not accompany the party heading south. They pledged themselves to the *Maquis* and asked to be allowed to accompany the *Résistance* fighters back into the hills. Jeanine begged for refuge for her family. She left with four *Maquis* without being promised.

Mrs. Roosevelt and Sarah Churchill were hurried to a camp in the hills, where for the rest of the day and a night they listened to radio broadcasts extolling the marvelous German advance into Russia. The eyes of Europe, even the eyes of the Gestapo and the *Milice*, were focused on what now would be called the Eastern Front.

By evening Berlin was claiming victory, declaring that the *Führer* had achieved complete surprise over the Red army, which was fleeing east in a rout.

The next morning a fish van was waiting—the same kind of vehicle that had brought Mrs. Roosevelt and Kevin and Vicky from Sète to Montrond—and the same three, plus Sarah Churchill, climbed in the back and settled down under tarpaulins for the return to the Mediterranean coast.

"Let us thank God," said Kevin, "that the German generals in Paris are so fond of *langouste*. They give these fish vans petrol and the passes they need to run back and forth across France, where almost no one else can go, so they can glut themselves with delicacies from the sea."

They experienced no adventures on the drive from Montrond to Séte. The next night they boarded a fishing boat and went to sea for their rendezvous with the *Skipjack*.

Vicky remained on the quay. She shook Mrs. Roosevelt's

hand and kissed her warmly and told her she would remain in France. There had never been any question of that. Mrs. Roosevelt held the slight girl in her arms for a moment and wished her every kind of good fortune.

"You are a true heroine, my dear," she said. "I apologize for any moment when I had even the slightest doubt of you."

The fishing boat wallowed in a gentle swell as it made to sea. It was stopped for a moment by a Vichy patrol boat, which confined its inspection to shining lights on the fishing boat and calling for an identification.

Not long after midnight the boat sat quietly in the dark, its engines throttled back so that it was hardly moving. And the huge black bulk of the submarine rose from the depths.

Lieutenant Commander Deakin came down from the bridge to welcome the First Lady aboard. Sarah Churchill followed Mrs. Roosevelt aboard the *Skipjack*. Kevin remained behind.

"Have business in Europe," he said to Mrs. Roosevelt, speaking to her over the rail of the fishing boat as she stood on the deck of the submarine.

"You are a wonderful man, Kevin," she said. "It has been a pleasure to meet you."

"Captain. Miss Churchill," said Kevin. "Would ye mind standin' back and lettin' me have a last *private* word with Mrs. Roosevelt?"

The skipper of the submarine led Sarah toward the hatch where she would descend into the *Skipjack*.

"Y're a wonderful woman," said Kevin to Mrs. Roosevelt. "In every way. I trust ye so much that I leave ye with a secret. Y've wondered what's in the black valise? Gold, my dear lady. Lots of it."

She knew, of course, but she pretended she didn't.

"What gold is this?" he asked. "It's General Rommel's. I am on a commission from him, have been all along. I'm carryin' his gold to Switzerland, where I'll put it in a secret account for him—

In case anythin' happens to him, he wants his wife and son to be cared for. I take a small commission, of course. Kevin O'Neil does not omit that."

"Where did he get the gold?" she asked. She couldn't help it. In spite of her emotions of the moment, she had to ask. "How could—"

"I b'lieve it was an Italian general gave it to him," said Kevin. "In gratitude for his not havin' reported to Berlin how the same general turned tail and ran durin' an attack. And the Italian? Well . . . They've been lootin' the world for millennia, have they not? Anyway, I am under contract to General Rommel to deliver his gold into safekeepin'."

"You are a remarkable man, Kevin," she said, trying to make enough voice for him to hear her.

"One more thing, dear lady. General Rommel did not bring a bodyguard to Montrond. Didn't need one. I was it. That's how I happened to have a Schmeisser submachine gun. Th' general had provided that. I found it under me bed when I found th' gold. So when I happened to come on a man tryin' to pick th' lock on the general's bedroom, I— Well, what could I do? I just happened to be carryin' a sash weight. Heavy things, y' know. Perfect for the purpose. The man had come to murder General Rommel, and I caved in his skull. If I'd known he was a British aristocrat . . . Well, now, I would have caved in his skull anyway. Vivienne, who spent th' nights prowlin' her hallways, came on the scene before I could hide the body."

"You are a complex man, Kevin O'Neil."

"Too complex for the likes of a simple, honest American lass like yerself," he laughed. "Good-bye, Eleanor. I wish we'd met otherwise."

"Good-bye, Kevin."

EPILOGUE

FOR SEVERAL MONTHS AFTER June 22, 1941, it appeared that Adolf Hitler's greatest gamble had succeeded. By November, German troops were within sight of Moscow. Literally. They could see the city from the hills to the west. They had only a few more miles to go before they captured the city.

Napoleon had gained nothing from taking Moscow. Hitler would have gained far more, since Moscow was a vital rail hub. If the *Wehrmacht* could have advanced forty or fifty more miles, Germany might well have won the war in Russia.

Committed to the battle in Russia, Hitler could not reinforce Rommel in North Africa. By brilliant generalship, Rommel almost, but not quite, captured Cairo and cut the Suez Canal. The British clung to Malta, and while they held Malta they could and did ravage the supply convoys heading for North Africa. Rommel never had enough—enough gasoline in particular—to win his North African campaign.

Hitler consoled him. Instead of more gasoline, tanks, and ammunition, he gave Rommel a field marshal's baton.

Field Marshal Rommel supervised the strengthening of the Atlantic Wall against the D-Day invasion. Again, he never had quite enough.

In 1944 he associated himself with the great plot to kill Hitler and end the war. It failed. He was so great a hero that he was spared the fate afforded other officers who had turned against their *Führer*. Instead of being impaled on a meat hook and photographed by movie cameras in his death agonies, he was allowed to take poison and was given a hero's funeral.

General Paul Rousseau died in 1944, shortly before D-Day. Jealous of his reputation and of the respect the French nation bore for him, de Gaulle saw to it that the name of General Rousseau became obscure.

Because General Rousseau had turned his eyes to another woman, Gabrielle in 1943 became the mistress of *Oberstgruppenführer* Karl Oberg, *Polizeiführer* for all of France. He was imprisoned when Paris was liberated in 1944. Gabrielle was stripped in public, her head was shaved, and she was marched naked and bald through the streets of Montparnasse. She married a fashion photographer in 1945 and became something of an artist at the developing and printing of photographs.

Josephine Baker left France shortly and went to North Africa, where she was ill and inactive for about a year. After that, she gave concerts for Free French troops and was commissioned an officer in the Free French army. After the war General de Gaulle personally awarded her the *Croix de Lorraine*. She died in 1975.

Gertrude Stein and Alice B. Toklas survived the war. Later they learned that the officials of their village had conspired to conceal from the Germans that the two old ladies were Jews. Gertrude Stein died in 1946. Alice B. Toklas died in 1967.

William Donovan founded the Office of Strategic Services, OSS, which in time became the CIA.

Hauptsturmführer Konrad Giesel, having risen to the rank of *Obersturmbannführer*, associated himself with the 1944 plot to assassinate Hitler. He was one of those who died impaled on a meat hook.

Kevin O'Neil delivered General Rommel's gold to a bank in Zurich. He went to the United States Embassy in Geneva and demanded his fee for safely escorting Mrs. Roosevelt to and from France. The money was paid, and he deposited it in his own secret account in Zurich—together with his share of General Rommel's money. In June, 1943, he died when a German airplane in which he was flying from Paris to Amsterdam was shot down by a British fighter. He was, at the time, carrying microfilm of plans for a German airplane that was to be built on a revolutionary new principle—a jet engine.

As Kevin had said, often as not friends muck up friends. The Germans found the microfilm. As a consequence, they captured and shot two British intelligence agents, seized and shot a German aircraft designer.

Jeanine Charlet survived the war, as did her family. Impoverished, however, Jeanine wound up working for the next eleven years at a job she detested and found demeaning. She was a uniformed housemaid in a home in Lyons. She was married in 1956, to the keeper of a tobacco shop. To this day, she can be found every day behind the counter of that shop, contentedly selling cigarettes and cigars and pipe tobacco.

Lucien Lenclos returned and claimed Château Montrond. Vivienne Duval returned as mistress of her father's home, which she inherited when he died in 1954. She married an officer who had known her husband during his imprisonment. She bore him a daughter when she was forty-four years old.

Viktoria Neustadt, Vicky, remained with the *Maquis* in southern France until liberation. She, too, was awarded the *Croix de*

Lorraine. In 1947, outraged by the episode of the ship *Exodus*, she emigrated to Israel and became as fierce a fighter for the *Haganah* as she had ever been for the *Maquis*. The British offered a reward for her capture. A Palestinian leader offered ten times as much for her death. He did not have to pay his money. She faced him on a street in Tel Aviv and shot him in the middle of the forehead with a tiny pistol she had concealed in her brassiere.

In October, 1957, Mrs. Roosevelt received a letter from Vivienne DeCombe, postmarked Fleurs, on notepaper embossed with the word MONTROND. Vivienne invited her to come to Château Montrond, for a week of fellowship and reminiscence. She would, she promised, assemble as many as possible from the 1941 group. She suggested a week in January, 1958.

Mrs. Roosevelt replied that she could not spend a week at Montrond but would come for a weekend.

The château was very different in 1958. It blazed with light every night. Floodlights on the walls afforded passers-by a spectacular night view of the ancient stones. All the rooms were clean and bright, the bedrooms newly furnished. Mrs. Roosevelt occupied the room she had occupied in 1941.

Within an hour after she arrived, she discovered something she had not expected: that one reason the château was so attractively refurbished was that some of the rooms along the hall and in the towers were occupied by paying guests. Château Montrond had become a guest chateau, like so many others down the river. In summer, nearly every room was filled, every night. Vivienne's husband, Armand DeCombe, was an accomplished chef, and the château was known for its cuisine.

Another surprise. An hour after Mrs. Roosevelt arrived, Vicky came.

"There will be just the three of us, I am afraid," said Vivienne as they sat in the small dining room, under the portrait of Françoise. "I invited Sarah Churchill and even Jeanine, but they sent excuses."

Vivienne had become gray and wrinkled, but her skin had regained its color, and she was still a beautiful woman. The fact was that in 1941 she had been suffering from malnutrition.

Vicky was the interesting one. She had aged little, except for a few lines around her eyes and mouth. She retained her characteristic enigmatic smile, a suggestion in her overall expression that she was perhaps, just perhaps, lying to you.

No, she said, she was no longer called a terrorist, was no longer the subject of a dead-or-alive reward. Israel had long since become a nation, and the struggle was over. She had not married. She probably never would.

After she had relaxed with a few drinks, she confessed she was active in an organization with a new mission. "We are looking for some people," she said. "Just looking for certain men."

"Who?" asked Mrs. Roosevelt.

"To name one, we would like to find Martin Bormann. We doubt he's really dead. Then two others, especially. Adolf Eichmann and Josef Mengele. I think we'll find them, sooner or later."

The next morning the three women stood in the rear courtyard, where Vivienne showed Mrs. Roosevelt and Vicky that the old well had been filled in. A rose garden covered the spot. A dozen mounds covered the bushes for the winter, but the roses were beautiful in summer, Vivienne said. Very beautiful.

"I am thinking," she said to Mrs. Roosevelt, "of writing a book. If I did, would you feel you had to deny the story from June of 1941?"

"No. I wouldn't deny it."

"Vicky?"

"I certainly would not deny it."

"Yet, neither of you has ever told it. I have always thought *you* should," Vivienne said to Mrs. Roosevelt.

"I imagine I shan't, really," said Mrs. Roosevelt. "You do it, Vivienne. The best of luck with it, too. Writing is not an easy venture, you know."

Vivienne nodded decisively. "I am going to try," she said. "I am hoping we can sit down this weekend and recall every bit of it. I'll make notes."

Vivienne DeCombe died in 1987. She had not written her book. No manuscript was found among her effects.